THE CLAN-LORD'S BANE

GALACTIC CLAN WARS
BOOK THREE

SAMANTHA CHARLTON

The Clan-lord's Bane, by Samantha Charlton

Published by Winter Mist Press

ISBN: 978-1-7385901-2-4 (paperback)

Edited by Tim Burton
Cover image created by Midjourney
Cover design by Winter Mist Press

Visit Sam's website: www.samanthacharltonauthor.com

Love and revenge collide in a battle for survival when a widow finds herself falling for the very man she's sworn to kill.

Isla can't let the past go. Her clan has won back their planet and settled old scores—but it isn't enough. She hates those she blames for her husband's death. She won't rest until the enemy clan-lord is dead.

And so, she sets out to kill him.

Elijah leads a powerful galactic clan. Furious that he has lost the planet his father only recently won back for his people, he seeks to establish order in his territory and strengthen his clan's defenses against their enemies.

However, he doesn't realize his true nemesis lies closer to home.

His own brother is plotting to overthrow him. And an assassin has just boarded his battlecruiser—a vengeful woman intent on killing him.

But the gods have a twisted sense of humor. When disaster strikes, Elijah and Isla find themselves stranded on an inhospitable planet. Forced to work together, they must fight for survival, not with each other.

And when passion ignites, they discover that the boundary between love and hate is a fragile thing.

Book Three of The Galactic Clan Wars series, THE CLAN-LORD'S BANE is a stand-alone romance in an exciting new space fantasy series.

"Vengeance is in my heart, death in my hand,
Blood and revenge are hammering in my head."
Titus Andronicus—William Shakespeare

In another time …
In another galaxy …

1. NEVER BE FORGOTTEN

SOME THINGS COULD never be forgotten—and Isla Mir-Brennan would ensure they weren't. She'd waited three long years for this moment, yet now the time had come.

Finally. After weeks aboard *Defiance*, the Mir-Ferrin clan-lord's flagship, she was ready to strike.

With determination in her stride and rage smoldering in her belly, Isla stalked from the landing bay. Fury had been her companion for a long while now, warming her whenever thoughts of Cathal surfaced.

Anger was so much easier to deal with than grief—and so she embraced it.

As she left, Isla cast a glance toward the small shuttle that sat at the end of the row of spaceships. One of the clan-lord's personal fleet, it gleamed a deep bronze in the harsh overhead lights. She had a keycard that gave her access to it, and she'd just made sure that the shuttle was serviced, fueled, and ready-to-go. No one had looked askance at her while she carried out the checks, as she wore a fitted bronze jumpsuit with the Mir-Ferrin crescent moon and twin crossed blades upon her breast.

For the past three months, Isla had worked as a technician upon the fleet of Arrows—the clan-lord's fighter planes—yet she had access to the shuttle bays as well.

That shuttle was her passport off this battleship.

She'd planned it all, down to the last detail. The day, the time, the place—and her means of escape. This wasn't a suicide mission. She intended to get off this battleship and return home—to her daughter.

An ache rose in Isla's chest then, guilt overriding anger for once. Reaching up, she rubbed at her breastbone.

I should have told her I was leaving.

Of course, there were many reasons why she hadn't—and things had been strained between them of late as it was. The truth was, Isla had neglected Bea these last three years. Physically, she'd been there with her, but emotionally, she hadn't.

Even so, she'd never been apart from her daughter for this long. The strain was starting to tug at her, like a long cord attached to her heart. The pull reminded her of the life she had left behind.

I will explain everything when I get home, she promised herself. *I will make sure Bea understands.*

Drawing in a deep breath, Isla squared her shoulders. She couldn't think of her daughter now.

Instead, she'd have her revenge—for them both.

Beyond the hangar, she joined the stream of uniformed personnel going about their business, her boots clicking on the polished white floor. Now she had to temporarily disengage the aft-shields, the weapons system, *and* the tractor beam—and she'd be ready for the next step of her carefully timed plan.

Isla wasn't supposed to be at work right now. Her shift had ended a few hours earlier. She should have been in her berth, sleeping. However, this ship was so huge that no one would recognize her amongst the sea of bronze-clad figures.

Leaving the landing bays behind, she took an elevator to the deck above, where she slipped into one of the many control suites that dotted the flagship. This one dealt with the shields and weaponry in this section of the battlecruiser.

Isla had studied the ship carefully. She knew exactly what she was looking for—what she had to do.

As always, the suite had a handful of officers standing at brightly lit consoles.

One of them looked up as Isla entered.

The man's lips parted, as he readied himself to question her, but Isla smoothly cut him off. "Corporal Misha Mir-Galbreth," she introduced herself curtly. "I'm a member of the Tactical Spacecraft Maintenance team."

The officer nodded before his gaze narrowed. "And how can we assist you?"

"The Chief Tech wants the shields and tractor beam disabled on docking bay 44RT for the next two hours," she informed him, holding his eye. "We're carrying out emergency launch testing ... he also wants the gun emplacements on that side disabled, for safety."

The officer glanced down at the console before him and tapped the screen. His frown then deepened. "Isn't that a shuttle bay?"

"It is," Isla replied, injecting an edge of irritation into her tone, as if she didn't have time for moronic questions.

And she didn't. Each step of her plan was timed to the second. She couldn't afford to be delayed at any stage of it. "The clan-lord's shuttles need testing ... just like the Arrows do."

The officer's hand hovered over the console. He still looked unconvinced, and Isla swallowed the irritation that surged up. Of course, there were some variables she didn't have any power over. The shifts of the control suite personnel changed frequently. She'd hoped not to encounter a pedant, yet Jidea, Goddess of Fortune, hadn't provided.

"Orders of Chief Tech Riker Mir-Ferrin," she added, using the name of the intimidating chief technician who ran the Tactical Spacecraft Maintenance team.

That decided it.

The officer's mouth thinned, and his fingers flew across the console.

A moment later, he glanced up, meeting Isla's gaze once more. "It's done."

"Good." She favored him with a brusque nod. "Two hours."

With that, she turned on her heel and marched from the control suite.

Two hours weren't long—but it would be enough.

The second stage of her plan was complete, and now she'd move on to the third: locating the clan-lord. A smile curved her lips as she strode toward the bank of elevators. That wouldn't be hard either.

One of the 'tools' she'd smuggled onboard *Defiance* was a small chameleon-drone. Only three centimeters in diameter, it had assumed the appearance of an eye-shadow vial while in her bag. However, when she'd set it free to roam the decks of this battleship, the drone blended in with wherever it found itself. In an instant, it could transform into a rivet, a button, or even a crack in the paneling.

And it had spent the past weeks floating through the hallways of the command deck, gathering intel for Isla. She didn't need the drone today, for she now had a clear idea of Elijah Mir-Ferrin's routines. And luckily for her, he was a man of habit.

The clan-lord wasn't one to lie abed.

He spent little more than eight hours inside his quarters, despite that he consumed all his meals there. The rest of the time, he was either on the bridge, in his office, or working out.

After leaving his quarters, he always went up to his private rec-facility and exercised for an hour. He'd then return to his chambers, shower, change, and go directly to the bridge for a morning report from his commanding officers.

Isla flashed a glance at her wrist-comm. In precisely fifteen minutes, Mir-Ferrin would exit the rec-facility and cross the walkway back to the bank of elevators.

Often, when he traveled the corridors of his battleship, the clan-lord was flanked by battle-droids— towering bipedal robots that Isla had done her best to avoid.

She wouldn't be able to get near the clan-lord with his metal bodyguards protecting him. And if she did manage to slip by their defenses and shoot Mir-Ferrin, they'd bring her down before she could escape.

But the chameleon-drone had revealed that the clan-lord never took battle-droids with him when he exercised.

It was a small window—and she'd seize it.

The elevator took her up to the command deck.

Access was restricted up here, but when Isla swiped her keycard over the control panel, she was allowed up. Misha Mir-Galbreth had boarded *Defiance* on Platinum 5 as an ensign—but once onboard, Isla had managed to steal herself a blank restricted access keycard, upon which she'd loaded her own details. Although Misha's identity was an alias, the use of Isla's real clan-name was a conceit that gave her a thrill. She'd married into the Mir-Brennan clan, yet she'd always be a Mir-Galbreth.

They were warriors.

And warriors never gave up. Their clan motto said it all: *Fight or die*. Isla couldn't go on knowing that two of the men—Elijah and Lucas Mir-Ferrin—responsible for her beloved husband's death still breathed. Cathal would be avenged.

The elevator slid to a halt, its doors whispering open.

Isla stepped out, her heart leaping at the sight of a battle-droid and an officer waiting to get in. The droid's crimson gaze slid over her before it stepped to one side to let her pass.

Head held high, even as her pulse thundered in her ears, Isla swept out of the elevator and into the wide corridor beyond. She ignored the curious glance from the officer and kept walking.

Early on, she'd discovered she could go most places on this ship if she looked as if she belonged.

Even so, the skin between her shoulder blades itched until she turned the corridor.

Swallowing, Isla reached down, running the palm of her hand over the grip of the slender laser-pistol she'd slid into the thigh pocket of her jumpsuit.

The weapon was small, yet it would do the job. Isla had smuggled it on when she'd boarded, hidden inside a lined compartment in her suitcase. She was good with a gun—and had spent the last three years ensuring her aim was deadly—yet if the laser-pistol failed her, she also had a laser-blade nestled in her back pocket. Likewise, the grip was smaller than most, making it invisible despite the form-fitting jumpsuit she wore.

She was armed. She was ready.

Heat ignited in her stomach, galvanizing her. *Elijah Mir-Ferrin is a dead man.*

Isla slowed her stride then, glancing at her wrist-comm once more. She was a little ahead of schedule. Although she had another elevator to take, she couldn't step out on the walkway too early. Surveillance cams would spot her anyway—but if she loitered, alarms would go off throughout the deck. Isla didn't want to give them time to send battle-droids up to the rec-facility.

Frustration tugged at her then. Of course, ideally, she'd have taken *both* brothers down today. However, the clan-lord's younger brother had remained on Platinum 5 when Elijah embarked on this sector patrol.

The warmth in Isla's belly started to pulse. The Mir-Ferrins were still reeling from their recent defeat against the Mir-Brennans, and these days their list of allies grew thin. She had to strike now—before they rallied.

Patience, she counseled herself as she turned into yet another blindingly white corridor. *It has to be this way.* She couldn't get close to the bastards on Platinum 5. Alpha Deck, where the ruling family lived, was too closely guarded.

She'd deal with Elijah first—and then it would be his brother's turn.

2. I KNOW WHAT YOU DID

ELIJAH BOUNCED BACK on his toes, just avoiding the sparring-droid's heavy fist as it swung at his jaw. Avoiding the droid's next strike, he ducked under its guard and landed a sharp punch into his opponent's heavily padded solar plexus.

If he'd been fighting a human, he'd have heard a gasp, would have seen his opponent double over. Yet the droid didn't flinch. It did, however, give a loud 'ping'.

"Disabling blow delivered," it rasped.

Smiling in grim satisfaction, Elijah stepped back and lowered his fists.

It had been a hard training session, but he was finally starting to get the best of the sparring-droid. He'd set it to 'expert level', and the damn thing had no mercy. It had pummeled him so hard of late, he had several fading bruises on his torso. Yet he wasn't going to let it beat him. Delivering two 'disabling blows' during a session was a victory.

Wiping sweat from his eyes with the back of his arm, Elijah moved to the rear of the mat. "That's it for today."

He'd cut the session a little short, although that fight had been an intense one—and he wanted to finish well.

"Yes, My Lord."

The sparring-droid—which was tall and lanky like a battle-droid, but with padded limbs and mid-section— turned and loped back to its charging station on the far wall of the gym.

His smile fading, Elijah shook out the muscles in his arms and shoulders, going through a series of stretches to complete the day's workout. He'd always kept fit and strong, but he'd stepped things up over the last couple of years—ever since his encounter with Vic Mir-Riorde. The cyborg had overpowered him far too easily that night on Platinum 5, and he told himself he'd never let himself be bested like that again.

Elijah frowned at the memory of the humiliating encounter. Of course, it was made worse by the discovery that Aria, his fiancée, had taken up with the cyborg.

He didn't like thinking about Aria. If he could go back in time, he wouldn't have sent battle-droids after her when she'd jilted him. Hunting down a woman who clearly didn't want him just looked desperate—unhinged. If she'd ended up with that cyborg, it was partially Elijah's own doing.

"Forget about it, man," he muttered under his breath. "It's all done with now, anyway."

Jaw clenched, Elijah continued with his stretches. He never missed a workout. It wasn't just about keeping fit; these sessions kept his mind sharp as well. The responsibility of this role was often a heavy one, yet he was determined to do it justice. His father had ruled their clan for thirty years—and had made it look easy—but it wasn't.

At the memory of his father, Elijah's frown deepened into a scowl.

Mican Mir-Ferrin had thrived on conflict. But Elijah knew he lacked his father's guile. He was as tough as the old man, yet he didn't have his ruthless edge.

His gut clenched then, the last of the euphoria of a good fight leaving him.

That's why you lost Idral. That's why your clan now stands alone.

He turned and stalked over to a bench that lined one of the walls. There, he reached for a towel, wiping off sweat from his face. Actually—although he blamed himself for losing the planet his father had taken back just three years earlier—*Mican* was the one who'd lost them their allies.

Idral, which sat near the edge of their territory on the intersection between the sector's busiest trade routes, had been his father's obsession for years. But when

Mican had launched a strike on the planet, stormed Mir-Brennan Tower, and taken the clan-lord prisoner, he'd lost the support of many clans who'd previously supported them.

And despite numerous discussions since, Elijah hadn't been able to win any of them back.

Was it any wonder when the Mir-Brennans launched their counter-strike, the Mir-Ferrins had no one to call upon to help defend the planet?

Elijah had taken precautions, for he'd known the attack was coming. He had eyes on the inside, spies who'd told him that the Jenna Mir-Brennan was planning something. They'd told him she was gathering her strength and had ordered the fabrication of arms. However, they hadn't discovered those vicious warheads she'd used during the strike.

They'd blown two of his best battleships to pieces and destroyed the new weapon installation that had just recently gone operational on the planet's surface.

Elijah dragged a hand down his face.

He couldn't stop thinking about that bitter defeat and what it had cost him.

The Mir-Brennans now had Idral—and the blockade around the planet consisted not only of their own ships, but those of their allies. Just the day before, he'd heard that work had started on a new Mir-Brennan Tower, built over the ruins of the old stronghold. Over the past years, Lady Jenna had taken refuge upon the Mir-Brennan planet of Staturine II, but now she intended to base herself upon Idral once more.

They'd never reclaim the planet now.

The knots in Elijah's stomach tightened. He knew it was hopeless, yet he couldn't admit defeat. Not yet. All the same, a hollow sensation filled him. Gods, he felt alone in this—out on a limb with the eyes of the Rith Sector upon him.

His wrist-comm started to vibrate then, the screen illuminating.

Cursing under his breath, Elijah tapped the screen with his forefinger, accepting a request for a visual connection. "Lucas," he grunted. "What is it?"

His brother's holo-image appeared a few feet away, flickering slightly as the connection between Platinum 5 and this battleship was established properly.

As always, Lucas was impeccably dressed, in a crisp bronze high-necked tunic and tailored black pants tucked into high boots. His black hair was slicked back, emphasizing his sharp bone structure.

"Good morning, brother," Lucas greeted him, a smile tugging at his mouth. "Am I interrupting something?"

"I just finished exercising," Elijah replied tersely. "I can't really talk … I've got a meeting in half an hour."

It was true—he did. Nonetheless, he wasn't in the mood to chat to his younger brother. There were only two of them left now, after their father and youngest brother had been incinerated in the blast that destroyed Mir-Brennan Tower. The tragedy should have brought the remaining two brothers closer, yet it hadn't.

Elijah didn't trust Lucas, and he knew the feeling was mutual.

"I'll be brief then," Lucas replied. However, the glint in his eye made Elijah tense.

He knew that look.

"Go on," he said, wiping off his sweat-slick arms with the towel. He wore skin-tight black exercise pants and a sleeveless top—both of which he couldn't wait to strip off so he could step under a cold shower.

"I know what you did."

Elijah stilled. A moment later, his pulse quickened. Nonetheless, he kept his expression blank. "*What* did I do?"

Lucas's smile widened. "I have to hand it to you, brother … you're the best liar I've ever met. It doesn't faze you in the least, does it?"

Elijah didn't answer.

After a couple of seconds, Lucas continued. "I found Doctor Varis and his team."

Shit.

Elijah looped his towel around his neck. "You did?"

"They've been mining ore on Galban 8. It seems on the night the lab blew up … the night Varis and his two lab techs disappeared … battle-droids yanked them from their beds and put them on a prison ship to the sector fringe."

Sweat trickled down between Elijah's shoulder blades now—although it wasn't from his hard work out. How the fuck had Lucas found them? "Really?" he replied lightly. "And you believe them?"

"I do. Varis insists that the battle-droids bore the clan-lord's crest."

Elijah snorted. "He's lying."

"No … *you* are."

Elijah held his brother's eye, even as his skin started to prickle. Lucas had just accused him of being involved in the destruction of the Starellusbacter—the super-bacterium Lucas had been working on for years. He'd finally 'perfected' his bioweapon, but Elijah hadn't allowed him to test it, not without a proven cure.

And when Varis and his team did develop antibiotics that could remedy that deadly bacteria, Elijah's conscience had kicked in.

He couldn't let Lucas set the Starellusbacter free on the Mir-Brennans.

If Mican had still been at the helm, he'd have done it—anything to weaken his enemies—but Elijah wasn't his father.

And he wasn't his brother either.

"You did well, disabling the surveillance-cams and deleting the research files," Lucas went on. His tone was still amiable, as if they were having a friendly chat—as if he wasn't accusing his elder brother of a gross betrayal. "But there was one cam you missed … you didn't know I'd placed a hidden surveillance-cam outside your quarters, did you?"

Elijah frowned. "You did *what?*"

"It seems you were out and about that night … wearing a hooded cloak," Lucas went on, ignoring him. "And you arrived back on Alpha Deck in the early hours of the morning … just before the lab blew." His brother paused for a moment. "That's a coincidence, isn't it?"

"If the person you saw was cloaked, how do you know it was me?"

Lucas laughed. "Who *else* has access to your quarters?"

Heat flooded through Elijah, anger twisting in his gut. "You've been *spying* on me?"

Lucas's smile slipped just a little. "Don't dissemble, brother." A muscle flexed in his jaw. "You *betrayed* me." Lucas's voice cracked then. "How fucking dare you?"

Their gazes locked. The holo-image was so clear it was as if Lucas were actually standing in front of Elijah, although considering the circumstances, it was just as well he wasn't. Moments passed, and then Elijah made a decision.

The time for subterfuge was over. There was little point in denying the truth any longer, not when Lucas now had proof to back his suspicions up.

"How long have you known?" he asked finally.

"Since two days afterward."

"And you've waited until now to face me?"

Lucas didn't reply.

Silence swelled between them before Elijah scowled. "You had to be stopped," he said, his voice hardening. "You were about to unleash chaos … and I couldn't let you."

Lucas's amiable expression vanished. "I should have been the firstborn." He bit out the words. "You don't have the balls to lead our clan. Father would turn in his grave to see what a mess you've made of things."

That stung.

Elijah already beat himself up about that daily—he didn't need reminding. However, he didn't let his discomfort show. Instead, he stared his brother down. "Luckily, I don't answer to him … or you."

"That's where you're wrong," Lucas answered. "As I said, I've known about Varis and his team, and about that cam footage, for a while now … but I've been waiting for the right moment to do something about it."

Anger spiked through Elijah's chest, his pulse quickening. "Don't threaten me, Luc. You won't like where that leads."

"I *know* where that leads," his brother countered. "To reckoning. Your rule has ended. Goodbye, Eli."

And with that, to Elijah's shock, Lucas cut the call.

Staring at the space where his brother's image had just vanished, Elijah blinked. "What the fuck?" he muttered. Had Lucas finally lost his mind? *Your rule has ended?* What kind of crazy talk was that?

And yet, it now felt as if a stone sat in the pit of his stomach.

He couldn't believe his brother had just threatened him, yet he had.

"I'll deal with you when I get back to Platinum 5," he growled as if Lucas still stood before him. And he would. The first thing he'd do when he returned to the space station would be to strip his brother of all his portfolios and responsibilities. The next would be to banish him. Galban 8, where he'd sent Varis and his lab technicians, needed a new governor. The planet was barely habitable; it was difficult to find those willing to live there.

But Lucas would rot on that cold rock; Elijah would make sure of it.

He checked his wrist-comm. His brother was a problem—but he couldn't focus on him now.

He had a meeting with his officers in twenty minutes, to discuss the unrest upon the planet *Defiance* was now orbiting. Elijah was never late for meetings, and he wasn't about to start today.

He yanked on his boots—for he'd sparred with the droid barefoot—and headed for the doors.

3. YOUR MOMENT HAS COME

EXITING THE REC-FACILITY, Elijah stepped out onto a covered walkway. Sitting at the pinnacle of the command deck, the clear tunnel led between his private rec-facility and the bank of elevators.

Layers of tempered glass lay between him and the bulk of Estradia—a tawny-hued planet that hung in the glittering void, next to its twin topaz moons. Like many planets, Estradia was beautiful from afar. Up close, it was reputed to be less so. Although it was habitable, the planet's environment wasn't a pleasant one. Stifling and overcast, with rancid-smelling air and frequent dust storms, the planet sat close to the edge of Mir-Ferrin territory, bordering onto some of the outlying Mir-Lelith systems.

Despite that it would never be a planet colonists flocked to, Estradia attracted those who shunned sector politics. It was far enough away from Platinum 5 for its citizens to forget they fell under Mir-Ferrin jurisdiction, and its governor had given the clan-lord no end of trouble over the years.

The planet's air was breathable at least, and settlers had discovered that the soil was mineral rich. As such, the few towns that pock-marked the surface had refineries.

But of late, there had been instability upon Estradia. Many followers of Wis had settled upon the planet. Devotees to the Seer of Truth were usually peaceful, yet these ones weren't. They appeared to be trying to establish a new order away from prying eyes. Reports had reached Elijah of street riots, vigilante justice, and retribution attacks between those who followed Wis and those who didn't. The locals were angry; they'd worked hard to create a prosperous, and peaceful, mining colony—and they didn't welcome the extremists.

Elijah was here to deal with the unrest, to shut it down.

Starting down the walkway, his gaze lingering upon Estradia's swirling surface, Elijah frowned. He needed to focus, yet it was difficult to do so with his brother's threats echoing in his ears.

What's Lucas up to?

Elijah was halfway down the walkway, still brooding, when the doors at the far end leading to the elevators slid open—and a woman stepped out.

He halted, his gaze narrowing.

Dark-haired, slender, and clad in a snug bronze jumpsuit, the woman looked as if she worked on one of the lower decks.

"What are you doing up here?" he called out, as a warning prickled the back of his neck. There was something about the stalking way the woman moved, the way her gaze fixed upon him, that stirred his instincts. "This is a restricted area."

The intruder didn't reply.

An instant later, her right hand went to the pocket on her thigh.

Elijah's heart jolted.

Gods, she was going to attack him.

Here he was, unarmed and without his battle-droid escort. She had him cornered.

The woman's face was impassive, yet her gaze burned into him—and even from a few yards' distance, he felt the sting of her hate.

Staring at her, Elijah also felt a tickle of recognition. Had he seen that face before? There was something about the high cheekbones, the shock of raven hair— pulled back from her face in a ponytail—and those dark-blue eyes that seemed familiar.

He couldn't place her now, and he had no time to search his memory.

Something else occurred to Elijah then, causing a chill to roll over him. Was this Lucas's doing? Had he sent an assassin after him?

Hands rising, he took a slow step back and then another.

There was really no place to hide in this glass tunnel. If he turned to retrace his steps, he was done for.

Silver glinted as the woman palmed a small laser-pistol. She raised it then, aiming at his chest.

"I've waited years for this." Her voice was low, husky, and triumphant. "Your moment has come, Mir-Ferrin."

Elijah opened his mouth to ask her what he'd done to deserve death at her hands. Perhaps if he got her talking, he could find a way out of this.

However, he never got the chance.

The battleship lurched—a deep 'boom' rolling through it. Metal groaned, and then the walkway tilted.

Elijah fell, scrabbling at the polished white floor for purchase as he went. He found none, for there was nothing to hold onto here.

Fuck! Had an asteroid just collided with *Defiance*? Were they under attack?

A stream of silver laser whisked past his shoulder as he tumbled, and he felt the bite of its lethal heat skim his skin. Despite the interruption, the woman wasn't to be swayed from her purpose.

Elijah collided with the closed doors that led through to the elevator bay, the air rushing out of his lungs. Gasping as pain lanced across his ribs, Elijah rolled onto his side. The assassin had also fallen against the doors, just a few feet away—and she still had her laser-pistol tightly gripped in one hand.

Like him, the fall had winded her.

Grabbing his opportunity as the woman twisted toward him, Elijah scooted in her direction and kicked the gun from her hand.

In response, she snarled a curse and drove the heel of her booted foot into his stomach.

Elijah grunted, falling back while she rolled sideways, drawing another weapon from her back pocket.

The hum of an igniting laser-blade, a white spear of light illuminating the listing walkway, cut through the groan of metal and the scream of claxons that now echoed through the ship.

Elijah scuttled backward and slammed his fist on the panel next to the doors.

The woman's blue eyes sprang wide as she realized what he was doing, her face twisting. She lunged for him, the blade slicing through the air, but it was too late.

The doors sprang open, and she fell.

Elijah very nearly followed her. However, he managed to catch the edge of the doors.

Hanging there, feet swinging into emptiness, he squeezed his eyes shut, readying himself to attempt to haul himself up over the lip of the doors.

A moment later, *Defiance* gave another deep, rending groan and listed back in the other direction.

Elijah flew forward and hit the floor once more, his belly sliding along its smooth surface. Claxons blared even louder than before, and when he scrambled to his feet, his gaze cutting through the layers of tempered glass, he caught sight of what lay beyond.

His flagship, the pride of his fleet, had broken in half. The stern now floated away toward the largest of Estradia's two moons. Its guts had split, its innards and bodies floating into space.

And then, as Elijah watched, his feet cemented to the spot, the stern of *Defiance* shuddered. An instant later, it lit up the void like a new sun.

Whirling away, Elijah brought up an arm to shield his face from the glare. The impact of the explosion hit the bow of the battlecruiser then, throwing him off his feet once more.

Heart pounding, bile stinging the back of his throat, he rolled to his feet and stabbed at the screen of his wrist-comm. "Bridge!" he barked. "Are we under attack?"

"My Lord!" The panicked voice of First Officer Erina Mir-Ferrin replied. "A detonator exploded on Deck 551H, splitting the ship in half."

A detonator. Had that assassin set it before coming for him?

"Where's Commander Yaris?"

"Dead, Sir. He hit his head during the first explosion."

Shit.

"There must have been more than one detonator." Elijah swiveled once more to the view out the window, where debris now swirled in a vortex before him. "The stern of the ship has been completely destroyed." He sucked in a deep breath then, trying to think clearly. "Can you seal the breach?"

"We've shut down as many airlocks as we could," the first officer replied then, her voice steadying as she regained control, "but many of the decks are too badly damaged."

"Order all remaining personnel to abandon ship," Elijah ordered. "I'll try and get to the bridge now."

"Aye, Sir," Erina replied. "I'm—" She broke off then before whispering a curse under her breath.

"What is it?" Elijah demanded.

"We've just located another detonator," the first officer replied, the tremor in her voice returning. "It's two levels under the command deck."

"Can you disarm it?"

A pause followed as she barked orders at one of her officers. And when Erina Mir-Ferrin spoke into her wrist-comm once more, her voice was flat. "No, Sir ... it's a pyro-detonator. And it's set to go off in just over five minutes."

Elijah's belly did a steep dive.

For a moment, he just stared at the glowing screen of his wrist-comm, trying to take this news in. And then he reacted. "Abandon the bridge," he ordered. "Get yourselves into the nearest escape pods."

"What about you, Sir?"

"Don't worry about me."

"Where are you located?"

"On the walkway outside my rec-facility."

A pause followed, and when his first officer replied, her voice was oddly calm. "There's a small escape pod on the deck below you, My Lord. Just outside the elevator bay. Take it."

With that, Erina Mir-Ferrin cut the call.

Elijah snarled a curse, grabbing hold of the edge of the door as *Defiance's* bow listed sideways.

He didn't want to abandon his battleship, but with a pyro-detonator just minutes away from blowing, he had a decision to make.

It seemed hopeless. Half his ship was gone, and he'd just told his officers to get off the ship. But he wasn't giving up—not yet. He had to get to the bridge.

Elijah moved.

Two other walkways, one heading to a viewing platform, the other to a meeting suite, intersected here. He glanced around.

No sign of that crazed bitch who'd attacked him. With any luck, she'd fallen to her death.

"All personnel, make your way urgently to the nearest escape pod." The first officer's voice boomed through the ship then, echoing over the wail of the claxons. "You have five minutes before this ship will disintegrate."

Elijah cursed. He was running out of time.

However, the elevator would get him up to the bridge in two minutes, max. Despite his orders, *Defiance's* first officer wasn't abandoning ship—instead, Erina was remaining on the bridge as she searched for a solution. He'd help her.

But when Elijah punched the call button next to the elevators, he found it unresponsive. Frustration wrenched his chest. He wouldn't be taking an elevator anywhere. And he wouldn't reach the bridge.

He was going to have to abandon ship, after all.

Heart pounding, Elijah shifted right then and yanked open the cover to the service shaft that ran alongside the elevators.

A cold, ozone-laced wind feathered against his face, letting him know it was safe to climb down. Not wasting any time, Elijah did just that, descending the ladder as fast as he could to the next level before letting himself out.

His battlecruiser shuddered then, lurching sideways.

And fortunately, Elijah found himself plastered against the round hatch to the escape pod.

"All personnel, make your way urgently to the nearest escape pod." The first officer's voice was back, flat, and resolute. Clearly, Erina Mir-Ferrin knew they were all done for. "You have three minutes until detonation."

Bitterness flooded Elijah's mouth.

This wasn't the way things were supposed to go.

This was *his* ship. He didn't want to leave it.

But he needed to find the fucker who'd done this—and he couldn't do that if he went down with *Defiance*.

Nausea churned through him then. *Are you behind this Lucas?* Surely, his brother wouldn't destroy one of their battlecruisers and kill their own people?

Jaw clenched, Elijah unscrewed the hatch and yanked it open.

However, he was halfway into the pod when someone barreled into him from behind.

4. CRASH-LANDING

ELIJAH FLEW FORWARD, diving head-first into the cramped interior of the pod. Despite that he put his hands out, in an attempt to break his fall, his chin caught the edge of the control console. Pain lanced through his jaw as his teeth grazed the edge of his tongue.

The same body that had shoved Elijah inside landed on top of him—a sharp knee driving into the back of his neck.

"I should have known I'd find you here," she snarled. "A rat fleeing a sinking ship."

Recovering, Elijah twisted, throwing his attacker off.

The woman sprawled back against the open door of the pod. A second later, she lunged for him again, her fist aiming for his throat.

They were all done for, but she was determined to take him out anyway.

Elijah threw himself sideways, and her fist collided with his cheek, snapping his head back.

The assassin had lost her pistol and laser-blade, yet she still could fight. Another fist jammed into his solar plexus, slamming him up against the control console.

Elijah grunted a curse. Fuck it. At this rate, they'd die locked in combat, with the escape pod still docked. "No, you don't," he grunted, grabbing her wrist as she went for his throat again.

Pushing himself off the console, he lurched forward and head-butted her, hard.

The woman went down, her eyes rolling back in her skull as she crumpled onto the floor of the pod.

There was no time to shove her out, no time to do anything except haul the hatch shut and slam the heel of his hand down on the jettison button.

The escape pod shot out of its dock, just as an enormous explosion rocked the bow of *Defiance*.

Elijah should have strapped himself in before jettisoning the pod, but there had been no time. The launch, and the explosion, threw him up, slamming him against the roof. His head hit something hard, and pain exploded in his skull.

A black curtain fell.

When Elijah woke up, his mouth tasted of iron and his head throbbed as if a battle-droid had just stomped on it.

Spitting out the mouthful of blood onto the floor, he picked himself up and clawed his way into the pilot's seat. Reaching up, he gingerly touched the crown of his head, where he'd smacked against the ceiling. The skin wasn't broken, and he wasn't bleeding, yet the throbbing was so intense it made nausea and dizziness sweep over him.

Swallowing hard, he strapped himself into the pod. Through the small window, he could see the ruin of his flagship.

All that remained of *Defiance* was billions of glowing fragments, a maelstrom of debris and dust. He couldn't see any other escape pods either, nor any Arrows or shuttles.

His throat tightened. Surely, a few other souls would have managed to get away?

Surely, he—and the assassin who was still slumped unconscious on the floor—couldn't be the only ones to survive this?

Queasiness surged, yet he choked it back.

Elijah reached for the controls, noting that his hands were shaking. His mouth thinned. Now wasn't the time to lose his shit. Jaw clenched, he turned the pod around and engaged its thrusters, angling it toward the only place he could go.

The glowing surface of Estradia.

Hands moving over the panel before him, Elijah tried to locate the nearest settlement. This planet didn't have any oceans—all water was subterranean—as such, he didn't have to worry about landing in the sea.

The display alerted him that the nearest settlement was a mining town called Scull Basin.

Elijah adjusted the coordinates for it.

However, as soon as the pod hit the planet's atmosphere, the instrument panel went haywire. They'd flown into an electrical storm: bright bursts of blue and white light streaked past the narrow window. The control stick jerked in Elijah's hands, and the small pod started to spin, veering off course.

He fought it, but the pod wouldn't respond.

It grew stuffy inside the cramped space, as the outside of the escape pod glowed red-hot. Sweat trickled down Elijah's forehead, stinging his eyes. Nonetheless, he continued to try and right the pod's course.

It was hopeless. He'd lost control.

It was only when they broke free of the heavy clouds that shrouded Estradia from the sun, and he spied the rumpled dun-colored landscape below him, that Elijah managed to right the pod slightly.

It was too late to angle it toward any settlements though. The best he could do was aim for the flattest spot he could find—not easy in the rocky, mountainous terrain below.

Reaching forward, he activated the landing sequence. The pod jerked as the drag chute billowed behind them, slowing their descent.

Nonetheless, the impact of the landing threw Elijah back in his seat.

The pod plowed into a shallow ravine, cutting a path through dull-yellow dirt. It came to a shuddering halt. The console let out one last, pitiful shriek then, and the engines cut off, dying with a high-pitched whine.

Elijah slumped in his seat, relief turning his limbs to jelly.

Merciful Syr, he'd made it.

Shifting his gaze to the woman on the floor, heat spiked through Elijah's gut.

Did Lucas really send her?

It seemed a coincidence indeed that this assassin had appeared moments after he'd finished speaking to his brother, and just before the first pyro-detonator went off.

Unfortunately, the bitch was still alive. All the same, she was the only lead he had right now—perhaps he could get some answers out of her.

She could confirm if his brother was indeed behind this.

With shaky hands, Elijah unclipped his harness, stepped over the still-prone body of the assassin, and released the door. The hatch opened with a hiss, and he pushed it wide. He needed to get his bearings and make his way to Scull Basin.

Immediately, a rank, eggy smell wafted in, and Elijah pulled a face. Ignoring it, he then stuck his head out and glanced around.

He'd never set foot on Estradia before, yet it was even bleaker than he'd imagined. Arid wasteland and the jagged outline of austere mountains greeted him. Nothing apart from the odd spiky bush or cactus sticking up from the dry earth appeared to grow here. The heavy clouds in the sky were a sickly yellow-grey hue.

However, the heavens were darkening; dusk was nearing.

Elijah's ribcage tightened. Apart from the woman lying unconscious a few feet away, he was on his own down here.

Survival was up to him.

Fuck it, he couldn't set off for Scull Basin in the dark. He'd heard most of Estradia's fauna was nocturnal—and dangerous.

Ducking back into the escape pod, he returned to his seat and attempted to switch on the instrument panel. It had died during landing, but surely, he could find a way to reactivate it? After several minutes of flicking switches, pressing buttons and screens, and adjusting dials, nothing happened.

Elijah muttered a curse. The pain in his head had settled a little, although the dull ache that remained made it difficult to concentrate. Looking down at his wrist-comm, he tapped the screen. Dead too.

If he wanted to reach Scull Basin, he was going to have to rely on his sense of direction, his instincts.

His gut hardened then. He trusted his ability to look after himself, yet he'd never been in a situation like this before—one where he had no back-up, at all. Usually, if he wanted things fixed, all he had to do was tap his wrist-comm screen or command one of his battle-droids and his problem would be resolved.

But not out here.

They'd been on course when they'd first entered the atmosphere, but then the pod had hit that storm, and it had veered east—which meant Scull Basin lay to the west.

Elijah tapped his fingertips on the dark console as he tried to calculate just how far they'd gone off course. They could be twenty klicks from the settlement or two thousand. There was no way of knowing for certain.

The knot in Elijah's stomach tightened.

He wasn't used to feeling out of control, to being so cut off.

Trying to ignore the discomforting sensation, he rose from the pilot's seat, shifted across to a locker built into the side of the pod, and opened it. Time to see what provisions he had to work with.

Pulling out the contents of the locker, he spread them out over the console. A large backpack was filled with a survival-dome, a glow-lamp, rations, canisters of rehydration tonic—a blend of water and minerals—and a first-aid kit. There were also some flares, rope, fire-starters, patrol hats to shield them from the heat and sun, and a laser-pistol.

A little of Elijah's tension eased.

Okay, he had provisions. He wasn't *completely* on his own. If he kept focused, there was no reason why he wouldn't survive this.

A soft, pained moan drew his attention then. Elijah glanced over at where the woman stirred slightly. When he'd head-butted her, he'd only immobilized her for a short while. Yet she'd clearly taken another hard knock when the pod had jettisoned.

Elijah's mouth thinned. She was close to waking. The assassin couldn't be reasoned with. The moment she awoke, she'd come after him again.

He turned back to the console, picking up the coil of rope. Since he was going to question rather than kill her, he needed to tie her up.

Isla's eyes fluttered open, and she groaned.

Her head hurt.

For a few moments, the pain was so intense that she couldn't focus on where she was, or how she'd gotten here.

She went to lift a hand to her throbbing forehead and realized her wrists were bound in front of her.

Raising her head from where she lay on her side on a cold metal floor, she looked up into Elijah Mir-Ferrin's face.

Everything rushed back.

Eyes closing, Isla groaned. "Shit."

The clan-lord didn't answer.

Isla's heart started to pound, sickliness washing over her.

I was so close.

Mir-Ferrin had been standing there on that walkway, unarmed and unescorted. Isla had been about to splatter his brains across the tempered glass surrounding him.

And then everything had gone wrong.

"I've got a few questions for you," Mir-Ferrin finally spoke. Isla's eyes snapped open, her gaze traveling to where the clan-lord leaned back in the pilot's chair inside the escape pod, watching her. "I suggest you answer them."

Isla remained silent. Instead, she focused on the long, narrow window behind him, through which she could see a craggy ochre landscape and a strip of dirty sky. They'd landed. It was getting dark outside, and the interior of the pod was shadowed, yet there were no lights on in here, no hum of the life support.

"Who are you?" the clan-lord asked.

Isla didn't answer. She wasn't telling him anything. First, she was going to find a way to free herself, and then she was going to finish what she'd started onboard his battlecruiser. After that, she was going to find a way to get off this planet and back to Bea.

Her expression must have betrayed her because Mir-Ferrin's mouth twisted. "I've tied those knots tight," he murmured. "You aren't getting free." Isla's jaw flexed as he leaned forward, holding her gaze. "I'm the only thing between you and death right now … so talk."

5. ABANDONED BY THE GODS

ISLA CUT HER gaze away, silently seething. The pain in her head was starting to subside just a little, and the strength was returning to her arms and legs.

Wriggling, she managed to push herself up against the far wall. There she drew her knees up to her chest, her gaze never leaving the clan-lord's face.

Moments drew out, and then he spoke once more. "Homicidal bitch …you blew up my ship and killed my crew." His voice roughened then, a nerve ticking in his cheek. The hands gripping the armrest of his chair tightened. "Three thousand souls, all dead because of *you*."

Isla's breathing caught. He thought *she* was responsible for that? Before she could check herself, she replied, "It wasn't me."

Mir-Ferrin leaned closer still, eyes glinting. "My brother hired you, didn't he?"

The question threw her, and she scowled. "No."

"You're lying."

"Why would I stay onboard while detonators went off?" she shot back. "I wasn't there to blow up your ship. I was there to kill you … and *you* alone."

He glared back at her—and then, as the seconds slid by, his expression changed. With a murmured oath under his breath, Mir-Ferrin sat back once more in his seat and shook his head. "I knew I'd seen your face before. I didn't have time to place you earlier … but I remember now." His brows drew together, his expression turning incredulous. "You're Cathal Mir-Brennan's widow."

Isla's lip curled. How chauvinistic that he'd remember her in relation to her husband. To him, she didn't even have a name. She was just the clan-lord's wife. Of no importance otherwise.

But he surprised her an instant later when he said her name, "Isla Mir-Brennan." His gaze roamed over her face before his expression hardened once more. "Did the clan-lady send you?"

"Lady Jenna has nothing to do with this."

She doesn't even know I'm here.

His lip curled, making it clear he didn't believe her.

Isla's breathing quickened. She didn't want Jenna to take the blame for this. In truth, her sister-in-law would be furious with her. Isla had departed without warning anyone, even Bea. They'd still be searching for her, would be desperate to know where she was. After three months, they'd all be thinking the worst.

Isla was sorry that it had to be this way—yet it did.

Jenna would never have let her go otherwise.

Mir-Ferrin folded muscular arms across his chest and stared down his aristocratic nose at her. "Why then?"

Isla's blood started to roar in her ears. Was he really asking her that? "You took my husband from me," she ground out. "You destroyed my life."

He stared back at her, his expression shuttering.

Isla looked away from him then, clenching her jaw as she struggled to contain her fury. Outside the window, the last of the daylight was fading. The cloud appeared to be lifting now, and the sky had turned a deep indigo.

Eventually, Isla broke the heavy silence. "I had everything planned," she murmured, still gazing out the window. "I knew your routine and had a shuttle ready for departure. If someone hadn't blown up your ship, I'd be on my way back to my daughter right now."

He didn't reply to this admission, and Isla didn't glance his way.

She'd said far too much. She needed to shut up now. Instead of engaging with Mir-Ferrin, she had to find a way to get free of these restraints.

"What a coincidence though," the clan-lord muttered after a pause. "That *both* you and Lucas tried to do me in on the same day."

Isla snorted. It was, although she wasn't about to comment on it.

Nonetheless, she hadn't realized there was strife between the two surviving Mir-Ferrin brothers.

She remembered Vic Mir-Riorde's warning then. *Lucas is the one to watch.* The cyborg, who now led the Clan-lady's Watch, had once served the Mir-Ferrins. Isla had ignored his warning at the time, but maybe he was right.

With Elijah out of the way, Lucas would take control. He'd also likely blame Jenna for this. What better way to rally the Mir-Ferrins against the Mir-Brennans—to throw the clans back into open war?

A war his elder brother appeared to be avoiding.

After their crippling defeat three months earlier, Elijah Mir-Ferrin had retreated to focus on problems within his own territory, yet his brother likely had a different agenda. He was the one who'd been developing that bioweapon, after all.

The deadly bacteria that the Mir-Ferrin clan-lord had *helped* destroy.

Isla's skin prickled. *Maybe I should have gone after Lucas first.*

Grinding her teeth, she shoved the regret aside, choosing instead to curse fate.

Dammit, the Gods had abandoned her.

Brooding, Isla leaned back against the rapidly cooling metal wall. A few feet away, Mir-Ferrin had left the hatch slightly ajar. Cool, rank air wafted in. It seemed the pod's life support system—indeed, all power—was dead.

Without the door partly open, they'd both suffocate.

As the silence drew out, and it became clear neither of them was going to break it, Isla emerged from the fog of her thoughts and focused on practicalities.

Firstly—where were they?

They'd crash-landed somewhere on Estradia, this Gods-forsaken Mir-Ferrin rock, and she had no idea how far they were from the nearest settlement.

Isla drew in a slow, steadying breath of the rotten-smelling air and tried to center herself. *You'll never get free of this rope if you continue to fight him. He's clever … but you have to outsmart him.*

Panic tugged at her chest then. She was teetering on the brink of disaster. One misstep, and she'd never see Bea again. Her daughter's memories of her would be a bitter, withdrawn woman who'd abandoned her.

She wasn't sure what Mir-Ferrin intended to do with her. He might decide to kill her in the morning, yet Isla's gut told her he wouldn't. She'd seen the calculating glint in his eye when he'd realized who she was.

No, despite that she'd end his life in an instant, he wouldn't kill her. Instead, she guessed he'd try to use her in some way.

Glancing over at the clan-lord's shadowed profile, Isla let the familiar warmth of her anger wash over her. It dulled the panic and filled her with determination. *We'll see about that.*

Elijah woke up with a stiff neck and a thumping headache. Neither was a surprise. He'd slept slumped in his seat, his head lolling back against the headrest. And after the knocks he'd taken the day before, his skull felt bruised.

Massaging the rock-hard muscles on the back of his neck, he blinked away the last remnants of sleep and glanced over at the woman who still lay asleep against the far wall of the pod.

He'd taken precautions before allowing himself to rest, and had leashed Isla Mir-Brennan to the wall.

Even with her wrists and ankles bound, he was wary of her.

The bitch was cunning—he'd noted how she'd adopted a blank expression after their exchange, yet he wasn't fooled. Isla was already plotting her escape, and he did not doubt that when she made her attempt, she'd go straight for his throat again.

She's deranged.

Clearly, her husband's death had broken something within her. Elijah wasn't personally responsible for Cathal Mir-Brennan's end. It was his father who had masterminded the strike on Idral and put Cathal on trial for crimes he hadn't committed—who had manipulated the trial so that the Mir-Brennan clan-lord was found guilty and scheduled for public execution.

Rumor was that Cathal had sacrificed his own life to bring down his enemies.

Lucas had demanded retribution for Mican and Tian's deaths, yet Elijah had focused his attention elsewhere.

And his brother thought him weak for doing so.

You don't have the balls to lead our clan.

Elijah's stomach tightened as all the old insecurities he'd grown up with resurfaced. *Maybe he's right.* He'd never fitted in—and the rest of his family had known it.

His mouth thinned then.

He wasn't above seeking revenge. There were people he wouldn't mind getting even with—but there were other, more pressing, matters to attend to. His father had left their territory a mess. Its fringes were lawless, its governors corrupt. The Mir-Brennans were the least of their clan's problems.

He might have lacked the Mir-Ferrin 'killer instinct', but he wasn't blinkered like his old man and brothers. Couldn't they see that if their clan continued to weaken internally, they'd be easy to bring down?

Pushing his self-doubt aside, Elijah heaved himself up off his seat.

One thing at a time. Right now, his biggest problem was staying alive. He needed to get to Scull Basin. Then he could focus on getting off this planet and facing his brother.

Elijah moved across to the hatch and shoved it wide before peering out.

To the east, the sky looked as if it were on fire.

Sniffing the air, he scowled. Gods, it smelled as if something had died out there.

Cold air feathered across his bare arms, and he shivered. Once the cloud had lifted, it had chilled off considerably overnight—something he'd need to take into consideration during his trek to Scull Basin. Fortunately, the survival-dome the pod provided had thick thermal insulation. At least he wouldn't freeze after dark, and the dome should also provide him with a modicum of protection from the planet's wildlife.

Elijah ducked back inside the pod to find Isla awake.

Seated against the wall, she was watching him, her dark-blue eyes veiled. The hatred he'd seen burning there the day before had gone, yet he wasn't fooled.

The woman was biding her time. She'd behave herself for the moment and wait for him to let his guard down.

But he wouldn't.

"Sun's up," he announced, moving across to the console and stuffing items into the backpack. He then threw Isla a nutri-bar, which dropped onto the metal floor next to her. "We can eat and walk."

"We?" she answered, her voice husky with sleep. "You're taking me with you, then?"

Elijah glanced over his shoulder, meeting her eye. "Of course, *darling*," he replied sarcastically. "You didn't think I'd leave you here to die, did you?"

Isla didn't answer. Instead, she picked up the nutri-bar with her bound hands, ripped off the wrapper with her teeth, and took a bite. She probably hadn't eaten in a while; it was little wonder she was hungry.

"I wouldn't sacrifice something so valuable," Elijah added as he turned to check that he had packed everything. Once they started their journey, he didn't want to have to retrace his steps. He strapped the laser-pistol to his right thigh, where he could access it easily when needed. "Right now, I need to reach civilization … however, once I return to my rightful place, *you* will prove a valuable bargaining tool." He paused then, glancing over at her once more. "Whether or not she sent you, I imagine Lady Jenna will be *desperate* to have you back."

Isla swallowed a mouthful of nutri-bar, her gaze narrowing. However, she didn't argue with him; they both knew it was the truth.

Elijah moved across to the hatch, tossed out the backpack, and shifted over to his captive, untying her from the wall. He then jammed a patrol hat—a military issue cap with a stiff visor—on her head before placing one on his own. "Time to go."

6. TIME TO STRIKE

THEY WALKED WEST, away from the sunrise.

Although the gravity was much the same as what Isla was used to, her feet dragged. Her head pounded, and she wished she wasn't wearing a cap. The patrol hat would protect her against the elements, yet it hurt her tender scalp. To make matters worse, the nutri-bar she'd eaten churned in her stomach.

She didn't feel like walking anywhere. However, since she had no choice, she followed her captor.

Around them, sheer rocky walls, the color of dirty golden sand, rose up to meet an overcast sky. The odorous air, although cool, was heavy.

Gods, what a bleak place. She couldn't understand why anyone would choose to make Estradia their home.

Shifting her attention to the man ahead of her, Isla frowned. Unlike her, the bastard seemed full of energy this morning. The clan-lord carried the heavy backpack with ease. Isla noted his long, loose-limbed gait. His right hand hung at his side, his fingers often brushing the grip of his laser-pistol.

He was on the alert, his gaze scanning the rugged sides of the ravine they traveled.

Isla's mouth pursed. She'd known that Mir-Ferrin liked to keep fit; however, she hadn't expected him to fight like a marine. Unfortunately for him though, she'd spent a while honing her own fighting skills. Back on Staturine II, she'd trained around four times a day, readying herself to kill the Mir-Ferrin brothers.

When she got free, she'd need to strike hard and fast—and this time, she'd best him.

And she had to get loose *before* they reached civilization.

Isla glanced down at her bound wrists. The bonds were tight enough to chafe the skin, yet not so tight that her hands went numb. Walking a couple of yards behind the clan-lord, leashed to him by a length of rope, Isla started to gently work her hands back and forth, in an effort to loosen the bonds.

However, a short while later, when her skin started to bleed, she stopped.

The fucker knew how to tie knots.

Seething with frustration, Isla glared at Mir-Ferrins broad back. She was tempted to try and take him down now yet checked the instinct. The heaviness in her limbs still hadn't worn off, and the throbbing in her head was getting worse.

Swallowing down bile, she kept her gaze on her quarry. The man walked with a purposeful stride.

Isla's shoulders sagged a little then, despair creeping in. Being held captive by the man she'd set out to kill had never entered her thoughts. There was a cruel irony to it, yet she couldn't give up—couldn't let him win.

"How far away is our destination?" she called out finally.

"I don't know," he called back. "A town called Scull Basin lies somewhere to the west. I'd set the pod's coordinates for it before the console went crazy and pulled us east."

"You've got a wrist-comm, haven't you? Surely, you can connect to the Sectornet?"

Mir-Ferrin snorted. "If that were the case, I would already have called for help." He then started to climb a hill. It was hard going, for the ground was dry and covered with small loose pebbles. Already his expensive calf-hugging boots were dusted in cloying ochre dirt, as was his clothing. Sweat gleamed on his bare, muscled arms. "We hit an electrical storm on the way down to the planet's surface … it fried all the circuitry inside the escape pod … including my wrist-comm." He tossed a glance over his shoulder then. "Yours is dead too."

Isla frowned, glancing down at her bare wrist. When she'd first awoken in the pod, she'd noted he'd taken it.

To connect to the Sectornet, they needed a device—a wrist-comm or a tablet at the very least.

Silence fell once more, and they walked on. At the top of the hill, they halted to catch their breaths. Isla gazed around her, taking in the view. They stood upon a wide plateau. The ravine where they'd crash-landed was far behind them now, and she could finally get a proper look at Estradia.

Rocky, dusty dark-yellow earth stretched for as far as she could see to the south and north, whereas to the west—in the direction they were traveling—the faint outline of jagged mountains rose against the jaundiced sky.

Isla pulled a face. The planet wasn't any more appealing from this vantage point. Nothing appeared to grow here, except for the odd tuft of yellow grass, a few sickly-looking cacti, and some shrubs with wicked three-inch thorns.

Heaviness pressed down upon her shoulders then—the emptiness of this wasteland was getting to her.

She cut her companion a sidelong look, taking in his proud profile as he surveyed his surroundings. Was the desolation affecting him as well? If it was, he showed no outward sign.

Mir-Ferrin glanced her way, and she dropped her attention to the dusty ground to his left. Her gaze alighted upon marks in the dirt, and she shifted over to them, crouching to get a better look. "Look at these," she murmured, examining the paw-prints. "We're definitely not alone here."

A shadow fell over her, and she glanced up to see the clan-lord had moved close. His brow was furrowed. "There are more prints over there," he replied, jerking his chin to the right. "Whatever they are, they travel in packs."

Isla huffed a sigh and rose to her feet. "Great."

They resumed walking then, heading toward those shadowy mountains. And after a while, Isla called out to the clan-lord. "No sign of Scull Basin yet?"

"No," Mir-Ferrin didn't bother to glance her way this time.

Isla raised her bound hands, rubbing at her throbbing forehead. She was extremely fit. Walking didn't bother her. However, her headache did. It was steadily getting worse as the morning dragged out.

She endured it for as long as she could before eventually conceding defeat. "Do you have any painkillers in that pack?"

Muttering a curse under his breath, the clan-lord halted. He then set the pack down, opened it, and dug inside, producing a small metal box: a first-aid kit. He found a blister pack of painkillers, popped two out, and approached Isla. He then scowled at her. "What's wrong?"

"My head is killing me."

"Open your mouth."

Isla did as bid, swallowing down the pills when he lifted a canister of tonic to her lips. She took another few gulps of the fluid afterward. It tasted salty and vaguely unpleasant, but her mouth and throat were painfully dry.

"We need to ration this," Mir-Ferrin informed her tersely, screwing the lid back on the canister. "We only have three bottles … and no way to refill them."

"And you *really* don't know how far away Scull Basin is?"

He shook his head. The clan-lord stepped closer then, his gaze narrowing as he surveyed her. "Are you dizzy?"

"No."

"Any nausea?"

"Earlier, but it's gone now … why?"

"Just checking you won't drop dead on me." Mir-Ferrin turned from her then, put away the first-aid kit and the tonic, and shouldered the pack once more. "Come on," he grunted. "We need to put some klicks behind us."

They marched all day, with only a brief rest as the sun reached its zenith—a faint red glow through the cloud—when they ate a nutri-bar each, followed by a few gulps of rehydration tonic. The daylight on Estradia lasted a long while, although, without wrist-comms or tablets, neither of them could keep track of exactly how much time had passed.

A cool wind sprang up mid-afternoon, bringing with it sharp needles of grit.

It wasn't pleasant. Nonetheless, their hats protected them a little, and the stinging breeze eased the suffocating sensation that had plagued Isla for most of the day. Earlier, the eerie silence, coupled with the acrid air that caught in the back of her throat, had been stifling.

The wind was at least *something* to break up the emptiness.

The painkillers worked, and the throbbing in Isla's skull eventually subsided. However, by the time the shadows started to lengthen and a fiery haze to the west indicated that the sun was close to setting, her belly had started to growl.

Two nutri-bars weren't much to walk on.

All Isla wanted to do was sit down and devour a bowl of spicy Idralian stew—one of her favorite dishes. But she didn't have that luxury.

Instead, all she could think about—especially as the throbbing in her forehead subsided—was completing the task she'd set herself.

Elijah Mir-Ferrin had made a critical mistake.

He'd turned his back on her all day.

The clan-lord still walked a few yards ahead, leaving a little slack on the rope that connected them.

Earlier, Isla's head had been throbbing too much for her to consider attacking him. Her captor had also been on high alert. Yet as the hours slid, and she behaved herself, she marked the way his shoulders had lowered. His back was no longer so straight, and his step had slowed just a little.

He was tiring.

It was time to strike.

Isla ran through her planned attack, move by move, in her head. She'd weighed up whether she felt strong enough, for she was tired too. However, she *did* have the energy, and she knew exactly how she was going to take him down. Her wrists were bound, but her legs weren't.

They were making their way down a slight slope toward one of the many gullies that carved the surface of the wasteland they'd traversed during the day, when Isla shot forward, closing the gap between them.

She jumped then, kicking out with a booted foot— hitting the clan-lord hard between the shoulder blades.

And as she'd anticipated, he staggered forward, knocked off-balance.

Isla pressed her advantage, slamming her body into him.

It was like hitting a boulder, for he was easily twice her weight, yet the momentum of the collision and the fact they were traveling downhill did the work for her.

Mir-Ferrin lost his footing and toppled forward.

Isla followed, grasping his hair with her hands, while her knees formed a vice around his neck.

The clan-lord bucked under her, his big body twisting. He tried to flip her, yet Isla held on. She yanked his head back, clamping down on his neck with her thighs now. She wished her hands were free so she could reach down and choke the life out of him. Her thighs were pressing into the muscles that ran down the sides of his neck. She'd immobilized him for the moment, but it wasn't enough.

Releasing her hold on him just a little, she waited until he tried to twist sideways—and when he did, she squeezed hard.

Mir-Ferrin gasped, his eyes snapping wide as her knee crushed his windpipe.

Isla grinned down at him. She had him. "This is for Cathal," she bit out between clenched teeth, while she leaned her weight into his throat. "And my daughter, whom you robbed of a father."

Mir-Ferrin's chest heaved as he struggled. Gods, he was strong. It was the frantic strength of a man who knew he was close to dying.

There was no anger or scorn in his dark-brown eyes now. Just desperation.

His hands clawed at her right knee, trying to pry it away from his throat, yet she clung on. Her thigh muscles were starting to burn now, sweat trickling down her back, but Isla didn't slacken the pressure.

She wouldn't until he was dead.

But then Mir-Ferrin flung himself backward, taking her with him as he skidded down the rocky slope. Grabbing a stone, he smashed it into the leg that was crushing his windpipe.

Pain lanced up Isla's thigh, and she snarled a curse, clubbing him across the face with her fisted hands. They were still bound, yet she could use them as a weapon.

Mir-Ferrin's head snapped back, but he didn't stop struggling.

He kicked out, pushing them farther down the hill— and before Isla knew what was happening, they were tumbling together, over and over, locked in a mortal embrace.

The side of the gully grew steeper as they headed toward the bottom, and once they started rolling, there was no stopping them.

Jaw clenched, Isla clung on as best she could—but the momentum of their descent loosened her grip on the clan-lord's throat.

Isla tried to keep hold of him, yet she couldn't. A shout of rage tore from her throat as she found herself hurtling away from him, toppling down the slope, unable to slow her descent. The sharp edges of rocks bit into her flesh and tore at her clothing as she fell.

Isla barely paid the pain any notice. All she cared about was clawing her way back to Mir-Ferrin so she could kill him.

But she couldn't slow her tumble, especially with her hands bound, and it was only when she landed face-down on the hard-packed earth at the bottom of the gully that she stopped.

The impact knocked the wind out of her, and for a few moments, she couldn't move, couldn't breathe.

It felt as if her chest was going to explode.

A rough hand grabbed hold of her hair then, yanking it backward. The next instant, someone hauled Isla to her feet and shook her hard.

Gasping for breath, she looked up into Elijah Mir-Ferrin's face. Like her, he'd lost his hat during their tumble down the slope. Blood trickled down his chin, and his chest rose and fell sharply as he dragged in much-needed air.

His dark eyes burned.

Sucking in a deep breath of her own, Isla launched herself at him. However, white-hot pain shot across her scalp when he yanked her sideways by the hair. He then shoved her onto her knees before him.

Despair slammed into Isla, knifing her like a laser-blade to the ribs. Gods damn her, she couldn't believe she'd failed. Again.

"I don't think so," Mir-Ferrin croaked, increasing his pressure on her scalp so she gasped. "That wasn't a clever move, Isla."

7. TOO MUCH TROUBLE

"*DEFIANCE* HAS BEEN destroyed, Sir."

Silence followed this statement. Lucas Mir-Ferrin stood in the clan-lord's solar, his gaze riveted upon the holo-image flickering before him. The commander of the Mir-Ferrin battleship *Conqueror* stood to rigid attention. However, his face was ashen.

The moment drew out, and Lucas schooled his own features into a horrified expression. "What?"

"The flagship was in orbit around Estradia when it … exploded."

"An attack?"

Commander Grav's long face tensed. "No, Sir … there were no ships in the vicinity when it happened." He swallowed then. "We've just recovered the flight-data-recorder floating amongst the debris … my officers are still going through it, Sir, but it appears someone set a series of three detonators."

Lucas's lips parted as he affected shock. "Was my brother onboard?"

"Yes, Sir … there were no away teams on the planet's surface when it happened."

Lucas sucked in a deep breath and put a hand flat on the polished desk before him, as if to steady himself. "No," he gasped.

"I'm sorry, Sir," Grav said hoarsely. "Your brother was … a good friend."

Lucas ignored his comment. "So, there were *no* survivors?"

"It's hard to tell. We were the nearest ship to the Velene System … and came as soon as we could." Grav swallowed once more. "It appears a few escape pods were jettisoned just before the final blast. We have no idea how many of them successfully reached the planet's surface. I'm about to send a team down to see if—"

"No need for that," Lucas cut in. "I will be there in the next five hours … my men will conduct the search."

Commander Grav's pale-blue eyes widened. "Sir? But what if the survivors are injured? Shouldn't we at least alert the governor at Crelcaster … he might—"

"No, commander," Lucas interrupted him once more. "Leave all communication with the planet to me."

Silence fell, and although Grav's lean face had gone taut with disapproval, he didn't contradict Lucas again. When he finally replied, his voice, although respectful, had cooled. "Yes, Sir … *Conqueror* is now in orbit around the planet. We're cleaning up the bodies and debris. If my officers discover anything else in the flight-data-recorder, I shall be in contact."

Lucas nodded. "Make sure you do, Commander."

With that, he cut the call. His brow then furrowed.

He'd never liked Grav Mir-Ferrin; the man was far too loyal to Elijah. Right now, Grav was useful, but Lucas made a mental note to rid himself of him once he was sworn in as clan-lord.

Standing there, alone in his brother's solar, Lucas let the seconds tick by.

His pulse quickened then, and he moved, punching the comm in front of him.

"Commander Starline," he barked. "Ready *Dominion* … we depart for the Velene System in half an hour."

"Yes, Sir," the woman replied crisply. "I'll have your shuttle ready to collect you in ten minutes."

The commander didn't question him—she'd learned over the years not to. His battleship was in orbit around Formidian—the massive uninhabitable class H planet that Platinum 5 circled.

Lucas terminated that call too and quickly made another.

He had to get down to Omega Deck, where a shuttle would soon be waiting for him. But first, he needed something fixed.

It took a while for the other end to answer, and Lucas started to drum his fingers on the desk, his heart still pounding hard.

Eventually, a man with an angular face, short light-brown hair, and sharp grey eyes appeared. "Good afternoon, Sir," the special ops commander greeted him with a satisfied smile. "The job has been done."

"It has, Nix," Lucas replied, his tone clipped. "But there are some loose ends I want tied up."

Nix inclined his head. "Such as?"

"All three of your detonators went off … but *Defiance* must have had some warning because a few escape pods managed to jettison before the ship exploded."

The special ops commander's smug smile slipped. "You think your brother was in one of them?"

Lucas snorted. "It isn't likely … but I need to know he's dead."

Nix's gaze narrowed. "I'll head to Estradia now, Sir. And deal *personally* with any survivors."

Lucas gave a curt nod. "See that you do."

He'd bought Nix's loyalty years earlier. The commander and his team had done a few discreet jobs for Lucas in the past. They were the best. Lucas wanted this done right. "Keep me informed."

"I will, Sir," Nix assured him, his pewter gaze shuttered now.

They ended the call, silence filling the solar.

He stepped out from behind the desk and strode toward the doors. A tight smile tugged at his mouth then. Soon this solar would be his.

For three long years, he'd stood in the shadows, watching while Elijah ruled, while he made all the wrong decisions.

Did Elijah really think Lucas wouldn't discover what he'd done? His brother removed any evidence that he was behind the destruction of the virology lab where the Starellusbacter had been stored—but he hadn't checked for hidden cams.

Lucas had thought his brother smarter than that.

When he'd discovered Elijah's betrayal, he'd wanted to take a laser-blade to his throat. However, he'd checked himself. Murdering Elijah publicly wouldn't earn him the position he craved. The commanders of the Mir-Ferrin fleet and the governors of the planets under their rule wouldn't follow a man who killed his own brother to gain his seat.

So, he'd waited. It had been hard, especially as he'd watched the Mir-Brennans take back Idral. In the aftermath, Elijah had focused on matters within Mir-Ferrin territory and refused to talk about what Lucas wanted—war.

But when *he* was in charge, all of that would change.

Outside the clan-lord's solar, two towering battle-droids stood to attention. "Escort me down to Omega Deck," Lucas ordered, walking past them.

The droids fell in behind him, the squeak and rattle of their metal joints, and the thud of their rubber-soled feet, echoing down the empty corridor.

Lucas's mouth lifted at the corners once more. For now, this squad of elite battle-droids belonged to his brother.

But when he could confirm Elijah's death, they'd be *his* to command.

Elijah folded his arms across his chest and watched the survival-dome inflate. His bruised throat throbbed, as did most of his body, yet he tried not to dwell on it. Instead, he was focused on ensuring he had shelter by the time night fell.

He'd set the dome down under an overhang in this gorge, which would shield it from view and provide shelter from the cold. The light was fading rapidly now, and the cloud was lifting with it. Already the air had a bite to it.

Glancing around him, Elijah frowned.

He wished now he'd paid more attention during the last meeting with his officers on board *Defiance,* when one of them had spoken about the wildlife that roamed the night on this planet. It would have been useful to know what he was dealing with.

His frown slid into a scowl then. That was a minor wish though.

He'd have preferred that *Defiance* still orbited Estradia—and that his crew all still lived.

And he wished he'd dealt with Lucas years ago. Blood meant something to Elijah, but he was a fool to care about such things. His brother had no such qualms about ridding himself of *him*.

Elijah's jaw tightened then, anger warming his belly. When he and Lucas stood face-to-face once more, there would be no second chances. And going forward, he'd be a lot warier of whom he trusted.

He glanced over his shoulder at where Isla lay, trussed up with rope, on the ground. The fire that smoldered in his gut flared hot.

Lucas wasn't the only one he'd underestimated.

His skin prickled then. The events of the past two days had done their best to humble him—and he wasn't enjoying the experience. He wasn't used to being on the back foot.

Isla's gaze burned into him. If he released her bonds, she'd come at him again. She wouldn't give up until she killed him.

His breathing quickened then, for he'd never faced down such naked hate before. As far as Isla was concerned, he'd personally put a laser-pistol to her husband's temple and pulled the trigger.

Like him, Isla was a bit worse for wear. Her bronze jumpsuit was covered with dust and torn in places from the tumble she'd taken down the hill. Scratches crisscrossed her hands and face, and a bruise was coming up on her right cheekbone from where her face had collided with a rock as she'd fallen; she hadn't been able to put her hands out to break her fall.

Elijah's mouth thinned, and he stifled a wince as his cut lip stung.

It was a pity she hadn't smashed her brains out on a rock on the way down. He'd taken her to use later as leverage against the Mir-Brennans, but the woman was fast becoming too much trouble.

Maybe you should kill her and be done with it.

Elijah considered the possibility for a few moments, his hand even strayed to the grip of his laser-pistol before he dismissed it.

No. Isla was too useful.

He'd drag her kicking and screaming back to Platinum 5, where he'd weaponize her. She'd go on trial for her crimes, and Jenna Mir-Brennan would make concessions to prevent her execution.

There were other ways to hurt your enemy, rather than tackling them head-on in battle. Lucas thought it was weakness, but he was wrong—it was *strategy*.

"Tomorrow, you'll be walking *in front* of me," he informed Isla.

Her lip curled. "Wise choice. Only an idiot turns his back on his enemy."

Heat flushed through Elijah, although he was careful to keep his face impassive.

Damn her, she was right. He'd been careless.

Elijah moved toward Isla then. To her credit, she didn't flinch, didn't break his stare. Physically, there wasn't much to the woman: although tall, she was slender. However, she was surprisingly strong and fought dirty.

Hauling Isla to her feet, he dragged her over to the entrance to the dome and pushed her inside. He then climbed in, sealing the dome behind him, and flicking on the power. A silvery light filled the interior, accompanied by a low hum as the heating kicked in. Moments later, the air started to warm.

Two sleep-mats had inflated along with the dome; they lay on opposite sides of the shiny dark-grey floor.

Elijah's gaze narrowed as he viewed the cramped interior. He didn't like the idea of spending the night in the same space as someone who wanted him dead.

Images from their fight flashed through his mind then. Isla had nearly bested him. There had been a few moments, as his throat had been locked between her thighs and he'd stared up into her eyes, when he'd believed it was over. His vision had speckled, had begun to darken at the edges, before he used his last burst of strength.

His whole body hurt from tumbling down that rocky slope—a lingering reminder of how close he'd come.

No, he wouldn't be able to sleep easily knowing Isla was watching him, waiting for her next chance.

If he wasn't determined to use her to his own ends, he'd have thrown her outside, let her fend for herself in the darkness. But she wouldn't likely survive the night.

Pulling out a nutri-bar, Elijah tore off the wrapper and took a bite. He then grimaced. This one was sweet, flavored like berries. It was cloying, yet he'd eat it. He was too hungry to care. Finishing his bar, he pulled out another. He then met Isla's gaze.

Her dark-blue eyes were narrowed as she watched him.

"Do you want something to eat?" It was a pointless question. Of course, she would.

Isla didn't reply.

"I'm not releasing your hands," he said, holding the nutri-bar up. "If you want this, I'm going to have to feed it to you."

"Fuck off," she growled.

"Rehydration tonic?"

Isla remained stubbornly silent.

He shrugged before sliding the nutri-bar back into his pack. "Suit yourself."

8. FIGHTING WORDS

ELIJAH STRETCHED OUT on the sleep-mat, stifling a groan as his bruised body protested.

Once he'd eaten and taken a few gulps of their precious tonic, he'd turned the glow-lamp off. Although the dome's walls were durable, they wouldn't prevent light from flowing out into the darkness. He didn't want the survival-dome to act like a beacon.

Elijah had his laser-pistol under his pillow, should anything come sniffing around.

However, it wasn't the planet's fauna that concerned him this evening—but the woman he was sharing this dome with.

A few feet away, he could just make out the lines on Isla's face. Yet her gaze glinted. Isla continued to stare Elijah down, reminding him that if she ever got free of her bonds, she'd make another attempt on his life. Fatigue swept over him then. Something told him he'd get very little rest until they reached Scull Basin.

Rolling onto his side, Elijah faced her. "Killing me isn't going to bring him back."

"No," she replied, "but it'll still give me immense satisfaction."

"For a short while, sure … but then you'll wonder what the point was. Revenge is a hollow victory."

"For you, maybe." She paused then. "However, I don't feel that way … and it appears your brother doesn't either." A goading edge crept into her voice as she continued, "He clearly doesn't think you fit to rule … and after you lost Idral so spectacularly, I don't blame him."

Elijah stiffened. Somehow, the bitch had scented his vulnerability and was now going for the jugular. She'd managed to flip their exchange so that, suddenly, they were talking about him and not her.

"Lucas would set this sector on fire if I let him," he replied, his tone clipped. "You better hope I regain my seat, or Jenna Mir-Brennan will spend the next twenty years fighting him off."

"He found out that you helped destroy the Starellusbacter, didn't he?"

Heat swept over Elijah. "How do you know about that?"

"Your ex-fiancée and Vic weren't acting alone. Lady Jenna sent them to deal with it. They told her everything afterward."

Elijah's pulse quickened, and his breathing grew shallow. This was news to him. When he'd gone down to the lab and found Aria already there, incinerating batches of bacteria samples, he'd been impressed by her courage—until she set her cyborg lover on him.

"Aria met Vic while she was on the run from you," Isla continued. "He took her to Staturine II, where she warned the clan-lady about what you and Lucas were working on."

"The super-bacterium was never *my* idea," he muttered.

"Maybe not ... but *you* sanctioned it."

"I did." There wasn't any point in denying it. A pause followed before he asked, "Where's Aria now?"

"Planning to hunt her down again, are you?"

Elijah frowned. This woman had a ready answer for everything, and it was starting to piss him off.

"No," he bit out. "That ship has sailed."

"It certainly has. Aria has Vic now ... and you don't want to mess with him." Isla paused then, her gaze glinting once more in the darkness.

Elijah's mouth thinned. If Isla thought that was going to wound him, she was wrong. Yes, he'd wanted to marry Aria once, but he'd never been in love with her. In the two years since he'd last seen her, any lingering affection he'd once had for his ex-fiancée had gone. The only emotion he managed to summon when he thought of Aria these days was resentment.

After that night on Platinum 5, he'd nursed a few thoughts of revenge. He'd even tried to track down the *CS Vertigo* and Greta Mir-Hamil—the woman who'd helped Aria and Vic escape—but the cargo ship and its pilot had disappeared, just as his ex-fiancée and her lover had.

Silence fell inside the survival-dome then, the soft hum of the heating unit filling the space between them. And as the seconds ticked by, Elijah decided it was time to turn the tables on Isla Mir-Brennan once more.

"You have a daughter, don't you?" The temperature in the dome seemed to dip just a little then. He'd predicted Isla wouldn't like him bringing up her daughter—and for that reason alone, he continued, "Beatrix … that's her name, isn't it?"

The light had faded further. He could no longer make out the lines on her face. Yet the weight of her stare pierced him.

"Do you think she'll be proud of you?" Silence followed this question, yet Elijah plowed on. He'd managed to stick a knife between Isla's ribs, and now he was going to twist it hard.

"I hope so," Isla replied. "At least, she'll grow up knowing her mother took a stand for something that mattered." They were fighting words; nonetheless, he caught the sudden brittleness in her tone.

Elijah rolled onto his back, staring up at the darkness. At last, he'd found a weakness. "She'll grow up an orphan."

Isla's breathing hitched.

"Of course," he continued, pretending not to notice her reaction. "If you do somehow manage to return to your daughter, you might not get the hero's welcome you were expecting." Cold silence answered him, but Elijah wasn't put off. "It's a bitter irony, isn't it?" he went on. "You embarked on the mission to avenge your husband's death … so you and your daughter could sleep easy … but in the end, this quest might cost you *everything*."

Once again, Isla didn't answer him. However, the rasp of her breathing told him he'd scored a direct hit.

A loud howl intruded then. The caterwauling echoed down the valley outside, ricocheting off stone.

Elijah forgot about tormenting Isla Mir-Brennan then, Instead, his body went rigid as a second howl rolled over them.

Isla's already racing pulse started to hammer. *Gods, what was that?*

She'd been imagining stabbing Elijah through the throat with a laser-blade and hearing him choke on his own blood—however, the noise tore her from her violent thoughts.

Her ears now strained to pick up any other noise beyond the walls of the dome. During the day, except for those paw-prints, they hadn't spied any wildlife. They hadn't seen many insects either, except for a few brightly colored dragonflies that flitted around them mid-morning. There had also been some clouds of midge-like insects floating around near dusk.

But whatever was out there now, it hid itself away in daylight.

Shifting position, Isla lay still, listening. She expected to hear something else, closer this time—but now that they'd ceased talking, the noise stopped.

Gently wriggling at the restraints that tied her wrists and ankles, Isla silently cursed.

There was no way she'd get free of these bonds.

Seconds slid by, and silence settled over the gully beyond their overhang once more. Isla glanced sideways then, to where she could just make out the outline of the clan-lord's body in the darkness. Her jaw then clenched. She couldn't believe she let him get to her. She wouldn't let him back her into a corner like that again.

Shifting onto her back, Isla stared up at the darkness.

Exhaustion pulled down at her, drawing her into its embrace, but she resisted it. She needed to stay awake, to wait until the clan-lord succumbed to exhaustion.

The moment he fell asleep, she'd strike again.

However, it was difficult to keep focused. Isla's body ached. Tiredness lowered her defenses and let despair in.

This quest might cost you everything.

Isla's chest tightened. Mir-Ferrin was sharper than she'd realized. She might have sensed his insecurities around his recent defeat, and his relationship with his brother, but it was as if he'd stared right into her heart and discovered her deepest fear: that in her hunt for vengeance, she'd lose the one thing that still made life worth living. Her daughter.

She told herself she'd embarked on this quest for them both—the Mir-Ferrins had to suffer—but the truth was she hadn't considered Bea at all.

Too late, she regretted shutting her daughter out.

The pain in her chest twisted sharply then.

Strike once and strike right.

Her father's mantra returned to her, causing her stomach to clench. How many times had he told her that? He'd drilled those words into her. Sometimes when she'd lost a fight, he'd shouted it at her.

Mir-Galbreths treated every fight as life or death, and her father was right. She'd had a few chances to kill Mir-Ferrin so far, but she'd failed at each one.

She couldn't fail again.

9. WASTELAND

A MUSTARD-COLORED DAWN greeted Isla when Mir-Ferrin hauled her outside, propping her against a boulder while he deflated the survival-dome.

In the morning light, his swarthy face was drawn and tired. Dark smudges had appeared under his eyes, his bottom lip was crusted and swollen, and dark-purple bruises had come up on his neck from the day before.

He looked terrible, and Isla guessed he hadn't slept much overnight. The threat of being strangled in his sleep had likely kept the clan-lord awake. Or perhaps he worried that he was leading them away from, instead of to, civilization.

They could die out of here.

Isla's mouth thinned, fear curling under her ribs at the thought.

Of course, she'd also slept fitfully. Isla had told herself she'd stay awake, waiting for her chance to strike again—but exhaustion had eventually dragged her down into its clutches.

Wriggling her fingers and toes, to relieve the numbness in her hands and feet, she shifted her attention from the clan-lord and stared bleary-eyed out at the red glow to the east. Around them, the gorge was empty. Whatever had made them nervous the night before had gone elsewhere.

Isla swallowed before wincing in discomfort; her mouth and throat were as dry as the ground she sat on. She'd refused food and drink the night before, yet she wouldn't now. If she wanted her revenge on this man, she needed to keep up her strength. "I'm thirsty," she croaked.

The clan-lord cast her a quick look over his shoulder, his expression shuttered. Opening his pack, he retrieved a canister and approached her.

Hunkering down so they were at eye level, he unscrewed the top and lifted it to her lips. "Tip your head back," he instructed curtly. "We don't want to waste a drop of this."

Isla did as bid, taking a few grateful gulps of the stale, warm tonic. It tasted like nectar.

Wordlessly, Mir-Ferrin resealed the canister and then pulled a nutri-bar from a pocket on the thigh of his pants. Unwrapping it, he held it up for her to take a bite.

Isla hesitated. She hadn't asked for food, yet her stomach betrayed her with a loud growl.

The clan-lord remained silent.

A moment later, she leaned toward him and took a bite of the nutri-bar. It was sweet and artificial tasting, yet she didn't care. She could have inhaled it.

Mir-Ferrin fed her the whole thing, waiting with surprising patience while she chewed each mouthful and swallowed. His expression remained inscrutable.

Instead, she sensed his worry—not that he'd ever admit such to her.

When she was done, he unscrewed the canister and allowed Isla to have another couple of sips. Satisfied that she was done, the clan-lord returned to his pack and put away the canister, along with the survival dome and glow-lamp.

Leaning back against the boulder, Isla watched him work, marking the sure, deft movements of his hands, and the way the muscles of his bare arms shifted and rippled. There was no denying he had a strong, sculpted body.

Isla blinked, heat washing over her. What was she doing?

Her face screwed up. Gods, she must be losing her mind.

"What's wrong?"

The clan-lord was now shouldering the backpack, his gaze narrowed as he observed her.

"Nothing," she bit out, even as she clenched her jaw so hard that her teeth creaked and pain darted through her ears. Exhaustion and frustration were clearly getting to her.

"Up you get then." Mir-Ferrin approached her in long, confident strides. A moment later, he slid his hands under her armpits and lifted her easily to her feet. Turning her away from him, he deftly removed the bonds around her ankles. He then gave her a gentle shove between the shoulder blades, moving her out into the gully. "Start walking."

"They survived the crash … all the emergency supplies are gone."

Nix stuck his head out of the escape pod to find Lieutenant Rena waiting for him. Her violet eyes were narrowed. "They did, Sir," she confirmed. "I've found tracks leading west."

Nix nodded before climbing nimbly out of the pod. "How far ahead of us are they?"

"A day on foot." She smirked then. "But we'll catch them up soon enough, Sir."

Nix's gaze flicked to the two needle-nosed hoppers parked a few yards away. They certainly would.

It had transpired that five pods had jettisoned from *Defiance*, yet only two had made it to Estradia—the other three had been destroyed in the final blast. Nix and Rena had already found the first of the two pods. They'd landed their shuttle around one hundred klicks away, near the ruins of the small craft. As Nix had promised Lucas Mir-Ferrin, he'd come down to the planet's surface to deal with this himself. Just him and his most trusted lieutenant.

Inside, they'd found three dead crew members from the *Defiance*: two human females and a Vulkar male. The pod had crashed against the side of one of the rocky mountains that thrust up from the surface of this jaundiced planet before dropping like a stone into one of the valleys below.

The craft had ended up mangled; its three occupants would have been killed on the initial impact.

With the first escape pod located, they just had to find those who'd escaped in the second pod to be sure the Mir-Ferrin clan-lord hadn't survived.

Nix was eager to get this job done, but nightfall had slowed their search. He and his team had planned the sabotage of *Defiance* carefully. They'd set the three detonators, hiding them deep within the circuitry, and masking them so that diagnostic sweeps wouldn't turn up anything suspicious.

The destruction of *Defiance* should have been the end of the job, but somehow, the detonators hadn't gone off in unison as he'd planned. Instead, they'd blown a few minutes apart—enough time to allow a few pods to jettison.

This was a loose end he didn't need.

Seeing his frown, Rena flashed him a tight smile. "Don't worry, Sir. We'll sort this soon enough."

"Damn right we will," he growled, surveying the stone-strewn valley surrounding them before his gaze flicked up to the heavy clouds that now hung overhead. The rotten smell in the air was overpowering this morning. Under the bodysuit he wore, he was starting to sweat. "I've already had enough of this planet."

His lieutenant gave a soft snort. They *both* had.

They'd been forced to camp out, listening to the sounds of the night beyond the walls of their dome.

Nix wasn't easily cowed, yet those distant howls had made him distinctly 'uneasy'. Likewise, Rena had been on edge for most of the night.

The coming of the dawn had been a relief.

The two marines returned to their hoppers. Climbing on board, they kicked them into life. The craft rose off the ground and lurched forward before roaring west, leaving a trail of yellow dust boiling behind them.

Elijah crested a steep hill and drew to a halt, giving the rope a gentle tug. A few feet in front of him, Isla also stopped, turning to face him. "What?"

He gestured to the rock behind her. It cast a long shadow and would allow them to cool off a bit. Although the day wasn't overly hot, they'd been walking for a while, and were both sweating heavily now. That concerned Elijah; during military service, he'd learned that regulating body temperature in a situation like this was even more important than conserving drinking fluid.

"Sit down," he grunted. "We'll rest here for a short while."

She did as bid, her face a blank mask.

Elijah lowered himself down next to Isla, his back braced against the warm rock. He then stifled a yawn. His sleepless night was catching up with him, and his usually sharp senses felt dulled this afternoon, his mind cloudy.

He took a couple of measured gulps from the canister before turning to Isla and lifting it to her lips. She drank thirstily, draining the remnants.

Shoving the empty canister into his pack, Elijah frowned. "One down, two to go," he muttered. "Let's hope Scull Basin isn't far away."

Despite that he'd just drunk something, he still had a raging thirst. He was rationing the rehydration tonic as best he could—neither of them was getting enough—but he suspected the town was farther away than he'd initially calculated.

They were traveling through bleak, uninhabited land, with no sign of civilization anywhere.

Worry settled like a boulder in Elijah's gut. Trying to ignore it, he swept his gaze about him and focused west on the mountains that steadily marched closer.

The day before, they'd been faint blue shadows against the clouded sky, but today they were becoming more substantial. He could make out the sweeping lines of the great peaks now.

"You're leading us in the wrong direction, aren't you?" Isla's voice, raspy with thirst, drew his attention then. It was the first thing she'd uttered all day.

Glancing back at her, Elijah scowled, even as his pulse quickened. "No."

"I think you are. There's nothing out here but dust and rocks."

"And Scull Basin."

"It's probably a thousand klicks away," she replied, her tone bleak. "We'll die before we get anywhere near it."

Elijah snorted. He then dug into his backpack for the pair of binoculars. From this vantage point, he had a clear view for several klicks in most directions. It was a good spot to check out the terrain.

Lifting the binoculars, he surveyed the western horizon.

A minute later, the weight in his stomach grew heavier still. Isla wasn't wrong. This planet was barren and unforgiving. Looking over the wasteland, one could believe that no sentients lived anywhere on Estradia.

Fuck it. She's right.

"Of course, you do realize your brother's going to come after you?"

Isla's comment caught him off-guard. Lowering the binoculars, Elijah frowned. "What?"

"Once they locate *Defiance's* flight-data-recorder, they'll discover at least one escape pod ejected just before the third explosion."

Elijah's pulse quickened. The woman's observations were unwelcome, yet accurate. It wasn't just dehydration and exhaustion that he had to worry about right now—but Lucas. It was another reason why he had to reach Scull Basin, and soon.

However, he wasn't about to admit that to his smart-mouthed companion.

~ 75 ~

10. A NOCTURNAL VISITOR

ISLA SWALLOWED HER mouthful of food with difficulty. What she really needed was something to drink right now. Not another nutri-bar.

The clan-lord was rationing their rehydration tonic strictly, allowing them both no more than a couple of gulps every few hours. It wasn't enough, and Isla's mouth was sticky with thirst, her throat scratched and dry.

Nonetheless, she doggedly ate her way through the nutri-bar, bite by bite, as Mir-Ferrin held the food up to her mouth. She was also getting tired of being fed like an invalid, although she knew better than to complain about that.

He was never going to let her feed herself.

The pair sat inside the survival-dome. They'd made camp once again for the night, after another full day's march west.

Tonight, there was no overhang to take shelter under. Instead, Mir-Ferrin had inflated the dome against the side of a boulder, so at least they were protected on one side.

In the light of the glow-lamp inside the tent, the clan-lord's face was as drawn and tired as she felt.

Heckling him earlier about taking them in the wrong direction, and about his brother, had brought her a certain amount of grim pleasure. However, she didn't have the energy to goad him now.

She just wanted to stretch out on her mat and sleep.

After Isla finished eating, Mir-Ferrin retreated to his side of the tent. Stretching his long legs out before him, he crossed them at the ankle. They'd pulled off their boots and left them near the door to the dome. He'd had to dress both their feet for blisters though, for two days hiking had taken their toll—fortunately, the first-aid kit was well-supplied with ointment and plasti-skin that would prevent the blisters from worsening and turning septic.

Isla shifted sideways, wriggling onto her mat. Of course, Mir-Ferrin had bound her ankles for the night, hampering her movement. Collapsing onto the sleep-mat, Isla couldn't help but let out a groan.

The clan-lord gave a soft snort. "Yeah … I don't think there's a muscle in my body that doesn't ache."

Isla didn't reply. There was a part of her that wanted to snarl at him—yet she couldn't summon the energy. All the same, she didn't like him talking to her as if they were allies in this.

"Isla," he murmured. "Can we make a truce?"

She cut him a sharp look. "Not interested."

Mir-Ferrin's dark brows crashed together. "There's a real risk we're going to die out here," he pointed out. "If you want to survive, we're going to have to work together. That means you're going to have to promise not to try and kill me in my sleep."

Isla glared back at him, anger and frustration knotting inside her. She didn't want to make any such promise.

Moments passed, and the clan-lord's mouth quirked. "I'm not saying we have to be friends. Just that you agree to work with me, instead of against me, until we reach safety."

She snorted. "And what do I get out of this 'truce'?"

"Waiting for me to fall asleep so you can strike, isn't a plan that'll get you far," he replied. "We're already exhausted. Why don't we both conserve our strength and focus our energy on survival?"

Their stare drew out. Actually, Isla *did* have the advantage here. She could sleep without fear of being attacked—but he couldn't. Nonetheless, Mir-Ferrin had a point. Continuing to fight him like this was exhausting her.

Finally, Isla cursed and rolled onto her back. "All right," she muttered. "A truce … for the moment."

"So, I have your word?"

Isla grunted. *Don't push it, asshole.* She then heaved a deep sigh, her eyes fluttering closed. She just wanted to go to sleep now, to shut Mir-Ferrin out.

Moments later, her eyes opened. "What's that noise?"

She glanced over at where her companion had shifted onto his side. His tired gaze met hers. "What?"

"That scratching sound." She paused. "There it is … louder now."

Silence fell inside the dome, and then the scratching, scrabbling noise intruded again.

Isla's skin crawled. "It sounds like an insect."

A few feet away, Mir-Ferrin's face tensed, his gaze widening. "It is," he murmured. "A massive one … with eight legs."

Isla scowled. "And how do you know that?"

"It's on the wall behind you."

Isla stilled. Then, slowly, she turned her head. And there, the bulk of its heavy pulsating abdomen pressing down against the wall of the dome, sprawled something monstrous. It was easily four feet in diameter—big enough to cover most of the dome's wall. And as Mir-Ferrin had warned, the silhouette of eight long legs was visible.

Isla breathed a curse. She wasn't fond of insects at all. It had been the only thing she'd disliked about going to live on Idral, upon marrying Cathal. The desert planet was filled with slithering, creeping, scuttling things— many of them lethal. And despite that Mir-Brennan Tower had soared high above the ground, piercing the sky like a great gilded blade, insects still managed to climb the sheer walls and get inside.

Isla had found a sand-scarab resting on her bed one evening. It had sat there, its blood-red carapace gleaming in the light of the bedside lamp, waving long antennae at her.

Her cry of horror had brought Cathal running. He'd turfed the huge beetle out yet had assured her that finding a sand-scarab indoors was considered good luck upon Idral. It meant Jidea, Goddess of Fortune, favored you. Isla had laughed the incident off, although her skin crawled for hours afterward.

Without thinking, Isla wriggled off her mat and across the floor toward the clan-lord. Oblivious to her mounting panic, Mir-Ferrin's gaze remained riveted upon the shape pressing down on the side of the survival-dome.

"Do you think it's venomous?" she asked, her voice tight. With her wrists and ankles bound, she felt vulnerable. She hated knowing that she'd have to rely on Mir-Ferrin to protect her—and he likely wouldn't.

"Could be," he replied. "I don't know much about insects though … I grew up on Platinum 5."

Isla swallowed. "I also grew up on a space station," she admitted. "I've never—"

A tearing sound filled the interior of the dome then, and a curved black claw burst through above her. The thing had sliced through the material with ease.

An instant later, it pushed a leg inside.

Isla's breathing hitched, her gaze riveted upon the flailing, hairy appendage. Gods, it was *huge*.

Mir-Ferrin breathed a curse and withdrew his laser-pistol from under his pillow.

Another tearing sound ripped through the dome as a second claw appeared. And then, a high-pitched hiss followed.

Isla's heart started to kick against her ribs. "You might want to do something," she said between gritted teeth. "Or it'll get in."

"Hold on," Mir-Ferrin grunted. "I'm lowering the energy output … to stun. That should be enough to get rid of it."

"Stun? Is that—"

"Get down … or you'll get hit."

Muttering a curse, Isla flattened herself against the floor of the dome. An instant later, a bolt of orange laser flashed across the interior.

The clan-lord had aimed for the underside of that swollen abdomen, and he hit it dead-center.

A screech shattered the stillness. Dusk had just settled, bringing with it the usual eerie quiet of an Estradian night.

The insect catapulted off the survival-dome and scuttled off.

For a breathless moment, Isla thought they'd indeed scared it away—but then another shriek rent the night, and it barreled forward, hitting the dome hard.

The wall bulged inward, two flailing, claw-tipped legs thrusting through the rips it had already made. One swiped, just an inch from Isla's nose. An overpowering smell of musky decay filled her nostrils.

Isla wriggled back farther, pushing herself up on the mattress next to the clan-lord. "Shoot it!" she gasped.

Another bolt of laser lit up the dome—this one bright white. It hit the insect in the abdomen once more, ripping a hole in the side of the dome this time.

The insect tumbled backward; its high-pitched wails and chatters rang through the darkness as it dragged itself away.

Breathing hard, Isla cut Mir-Ferrin a sideways glance. "It nearly had us," she panted. "You should have set your weapon to 'kill' the first time."

Mir-Ferrin's face was ashen in the light of the glow-lamp overhead. "Don't worry, I had the situation in hand," he muttered.

"Sure, you did."

High spots of color now rose to his cheeks, replacing the pallor. She'd managed to embarrass him. However, when he replied, his tone was cutting, "You're alive, aren't you?" His gaze narrowed then. "You can climb off me now."

Isla went rigid. She then realized that, indeed, she was practically sitting on the clan-lord's lap. Her thighs were across his, and the heat of his body soaked into her through their layers of clothing.

Her own face burning now, she jerked herself away, as if stung, and scooted back over to her side of the dome.

Elijah coughed as the chill, bitter air that wafted into the interior through three gaping holes caught in his throat. Eying the damage to the dome, he moved to his pack. He needed to find something to repair the holes with, or they'd likely die of exposure overnight.

During the day, Estradia's air was stifling—but at night, the temperature dropped dramatically. Elijah had noted that Isla was now shivering. Predators aside, the survival-dome, with its thermal insulation and heating unit, was a necessity for humans after dark here.

Elijah holstered his laser-pistol on his thigh. He then extracted a small kit from a side pocket of the pack and removed some adhesive patches. Shifting past Isla, he set about repairing the holes in the survival-dome.

In truth, he was grateful to have something to focus on. His heart was still pounding after that near miss, and he was sweating heavily—not just from fear but embarrassment.

Idiot. Isla was right: his hesitation had nearly cost them both dearly.

My father wouldn't have hesitated. The thought rose, unbidden, and Elijah's stomach tightened. No, and neither would either of his brothers.

But he had. His first instinct had been to preserve life rather than take it—and it had almost gotten them killed.

You don't have the balls to lead our clan.

Once again, Lucas's voice heckled him. Jaw clenched, Elijah pushed aside the unwelcome thoughts and concentrated on repairing the dome.

The kit wasn't big—and it took every patch in it to seal up the tears. Nonetheless, he managed. Sitting back on his haunches, he surveyed his work. It wasn't neat, but it was done.

He then reached overhead and switched off the glow-lamp. Meanwhile, Isla had turned on her side, her back to him.

Elijah's gaze settled upon her, and he frowned. "You'd better have my sleep-mat," he said gruffly. "It's protected by the boulder … and should we get any other visitors, I'm better equipped to deal with them."

Isla muttered something under her breath and wriggled off her mat. She then rolled across to his one.

Wordlessly, he pulled his pack over to the other side of the dome before stretching out on the sleep-mat there.

Silence fell, the comforting hum of the heating unit filling the dome. Now that Elijah had fixed the holes in the wall, the air had warmed in here once more.

Outdoors, a long, drawn-out wail split the night.

Reaching down, Elijah brushed his fingertips across the grip of his laser-pistol. He'd be sleeping with the weapon within easy reach tonight.

11. COLLATERAL DAMAGE

NIX LOWERED HIS binoculars, his mouth compressing into a line. "I don't believe it … the bastard survived."

Next to him, Lieutenant Rena made a sound low in her throat. "What, Sir? Elijah Mir-Ferrin's alive?"

Nix nodded, passing her the binoculars. "Face recognition is a match."

His companion lifted the field glasses to her eyes and peered west. A couple of klicks away, two tiny figures stood upon a high ridge. They were barely noticeable, and if Nix hadn't been scanning the horizon with his binoculars, he wouldn't have seen them.

"Raul's balls," Rena growled. "That's Mir-Ferrin all right." She paused then. "Who's the woman with him?"

"Who cares … she's collateral damage." Nix's pulse quickened just a little. "How the fuck did *he* manage to escape that blast?" A chill rippled down his spine then. Lucas wouldn't be happy about this.

"He must have been near an escape pod," Rena replied, still staring into the binoculars. "As the detonators didn't go off simultaneously, he had time to flee."

Nix frowned. He didn't need reminding of the mistake. When this was over, members of his team would answer for this mess.

"Hang on, Sir," his lieutenant continued before he could answer. "The woman's hands are bound behind her back … she's his *prisoner*."

Nix's frown deepened. Now that *was* odd. "Good," he murmured after a beat. "That'll slow them both down … and make them easier to kill."

Elijah screwed on the lid tightly. Gods, he was thirsty. His throat was cracked and dry. He desperately wanted to gulp down the tonic, yet this canister only had around two inches of liquid left in the bottom.

After that, they just had one more left.

Elijah's breathing grew shallow. They were halfway through their third day's journey west, and still there was no sign of their destination. The mountains were close now, their sheer yellow-brown sides looming into the sky.

Upon cresting the ridge, they'd stopped to survey their surroundings before sitting down in the shade of a rock overhang. It was a resting place that gave them a view southeast, across the vast plain they'd just traversed.

"There's dust rising in the distance," Isla said then, her voice husky.

Glancing up, Elijah followed her gaze across the plain below them.

And sure enough, he too spied twin plumes of dust.

Grabbing his binoculars, he leaned forward, scanning the view. A couple of seconds later, he spied two figures crouched over the handlebars of their hoppers, speeding toward them.

At this distance, he couldn't make out the faces of the riders. They could have been human, although the protective googles they wore made it difficult to tell. Both figures were lean and had what looked like dark-grey and bronze body armor.

The skin on the back of his neck prickled as he lowered the binoculars. "Two hoppers traveling straight for us," he murmured.

"Friend or foe?"

"They're wearing Mir-Ferrin colors."

Isla swore under her breath. "They're moving fast," she observed.

She was right. The hoppers roared toward them like twin pyro-torpedoes locked in on a target. They were seated now, but earlier they'd been highly visible up here on the ridge.

Elijah got to his feet and hauled her up after him. "If I had to guess, I'd say those two aren't here to rescue me," he announced.

"Right then." Isla's expression hardened. "What are you going to do?"

"Get off this ridge for starters," he replied, putting the binoculars away and shouldering his pack. He then gave the leash that bound them a tug. "Come on."

"Running won't help," Isla muttered, moving ahead of him at a jog. "They're on hoppers, remember?"

"We aren't running," he replied. "We're looking for cover."

The ridge sloped down to a high plateau—one studded with a sea of sharp-edged boulders and rocks. Weaving into the midst of them, Elijah pulled Isla behind a boulder and shrugged off his pack. He then drew his laser-pistol and set the energy output to maximum.

He'd learned his lesson last night. This time, he'd be shooting to kill.

"I hope you've got a good aim with that thing," Isla quipped. "Fast-moving targets aren't easy to hit."

Elijah shot her an irritated look. "I know what I'm doing." He *was* good with a laser-pistol. He'd trained regularly over the years, although he'd never been in real close combat before. His gut tightened at the reminder.

Meanwhile, Isla's gaze never wavered. "You need to free me, Mir-Ferrin."

He snorted. "No." Elijah moved to the edge of the boulder and peered up the gentle slope toward the top of the ridge. No sign of the hoppers, yet. "That's not happening."

"I'm no good to you with my hands bound."

"Maybe … but I'm not having you club me over the back of the head with a rock while I'm focused elsewhere."

"I won't." Something in her tone made him turn to Isla once more. She was watching him, her expression fierce. A nerve ticked in her cheek. "I thought we had a truce?"

Elijah cocked an eyebrow. "We do … but that didn't include me untying you."

"But I can't defend myself with my hands bound."

"Don't worry," he replied, flashing her a bitter smile. "It's me they want."

"That doesn't matter." She bit the words out. "They'll kill me too."

Elijah peered around the edge of the boulder once more. Still no sign of the hoppers—yet he knew they were close. His heart was pounding now, sweat trickling down between his shoulder blades.

"Even if I was to release your wrists, you don't have anything to defend yourself with," he pointed out then. Gods, he couldn't believe he was even entertaining this.

"No … but at least I can fight," she shot back. "With my hands bound, I'm a dead woman."

Swearing under his breath, Elijah shifted close, holstered his laser-pistol a moment, and deftly released her wrists. And as he did so, his gaze speared hers. "Try anything and it'll be *me* that kills you," he warned softly. He meant it too. As valuable as this woman was as leverage against the Mir-Brennans, he was now out of patience.

Isla gave a curt nod.

The rope fell away, and Elijah took a smart step back from her, drawing his gun once more.

Casting her a final warning glance, he shifted to the edge of the boulder and carefully peered toward the top of the ridge. And as his gaze settled upon it, two gleaming silver hoppers crested the edge. "Here they come."

"So … you have a plan, I take it?" Isla asked, her voice tight. She was standing next to him now, her gaze trained on the two craft. They'd barreled over the top of the ridge, but upon not seeing their quarry up ahead, the hoppers slowed.

Elijah's fingers flexed upon the grip of his laser-pistol. "Maybe."

"They're both human," she replied. "One male and one female … and you were right, they're wearing Mir-Ferrin military-grade body armor."

"They're armed too," he muttered. "Laser-pistols on their right thighs … and utility belts around their waists."

"The man has just drawn his pistol."

"Right." Elijah raised his own weapon and squinted into the distance. "They should be in range in around twenty seconds."

"They've slowed their speed," Isla warned him then.

"Noted." His finger flexed on the trigger. "They haven't seen us yet though."

Indeed, both the bronze-clad figures were still scanning the rocks to the north.

Elijah sighted his pistol on the male.

"Aim for his chest," Isla whispered. "The head is too hard to hit at this range."

"I know that," he snapped, irritated. "Although that body-armor is tough … a strike to the chest won't kill him."

"No, but it'll knock him off his hopper," Isla replied. "We're almost there. Three … two … one … go."

Elijah stilled his breathing, narrowed his gaze, and gently squeezed the trigger.

A volley of silver laser ripped through the dusty air and hit the male rider directly in the breastbone. And the blast toppled him straight off his hopper.

"Good shot," she murmured.

However, Elijah was already sighting the second rider.

An instant later, he fired once more. Unfortunately, that shot went wide. He'd had the element of surprise earlier, but no longer. Meanwhile, the man was picking himself up off the ground.

As Elijah had predicted, even though the chest of his suit of body armor was scorched, the bastard was still alive. A few yards away, the hopper bounced to a halt, hovering above the dusty ground, its engine idling.

Elijah shot at the man again. But despite that he'd just taken a hit to the chest and fallen backward off his hopper, the lithe figure dove out of the way and took cover behind a rock.

An instant later, laser plowed into the ground next to Elijah. Slamming himself up against the side of the boulder, he glanced over at Isla. In the absence of any other weapon, she'd picked up a stone, one that fitted neatly into her palm.

Her face was set in an expression he'd come to know well in the past few days: grim determination. "We need to pick them off separately," she announced then. "I'll go after the male … you try and shoot the female down when she gets closer."

Elijah nodded. This time, her assertiveness didn't irritate him. If they were going to survive the next minute or so, they needed to work together.

Isla knew what she was doing in a fight; she'd already demonstrated that.

Dropping into a crouch, Elijah shifted back to the edge of the boulder, ducked out, and shot at the female hopper rider once more. She was coming at him fast now, crouched low over the handlebars.

She'd holstered her own weapon—deciding instead to run him down.

Protective eye goggles glinting, she maneuvered the hopper close to the ground, tilting it left and right as he fired volley after volley of laser.

Elijah held his ground. He continued to shoot while she rocketed toward him.

A bolt caught the front of the hopper, causing the craft to veer to the right. Seizing his chance, Elijah moved out from his cover and fired again.

He hit the woman in the shoulder, yet it didn't dislodge her from her seat. Face contorted, she drew something from her utility belt and tossed it at him.

Elijah dived side-ways, flattening himself on the ground behind the boulder as an explosion caused the earth to tremble. Dust and shards of rock rained down on him, peppering any exposed skin.

Cursing, Elijah scrabbled forward, his ears ringing.

She'd just lobbed a pyro-detonator at him.

When he tried to get up, he staggered and was forced to brace himself against the boulder for a second or two. The explosion had knocked him off balance. His ears throbbed, and his eyes stung from the dust. However, he still gripped his laser-pistol.

Stumbling forward, he made his way to the far side of the boulder, ducking around the edge.

That was a mistake, for a booted foot kicked out, knocking the laser-pistol from Elijah's hand. Another vicious kick caught him in the chest.

Elijah sprawled, landing on his back in the dust.

The woman, who'd abandoned her hopper to fight on foot, stood before him, weapon raised.

Elijah's blood started to roar in his ears.

Fuck. He was done for.

12. DEAD AND GONE

TIME SLOWED.

ELIJAH scrabbled back, sharp stones digging into his palms. But he didn't take his gaze off the woman.

A small victory smile stretched her lips. It was over for him; they both knew it.

Elijah stared back at her and waited for a blast of laser to hit him in the chest. Unlike their attackers, he wasn't wearing body armor. A laser bolt at close range would burn a hole through him.

But the shot never came.

Instead, the woman lurched sideways, a sharp cry tearing from her throat. A bolt of laser went wide, no more than a foot from Elijah.

A stone had just struck his assailant hard on the head.

Seizing his brief reprieve, Elijah moved.

Rolling sideways, he reached for the laser-pistol she'd kicked from his hand. He righted himself as she came for him again and shot her twice, at close range, in the chest.

The woman crumpled.

His gaze cut left, to where a slender figure clad in bronze streaked from rock to rock.

Isla had a good throwing arm on her.

Elijah surveyed his surroundings, gaze narrowing. The second attacker was nowhere to be seen.

Elijah shifted toward the hopper the woman had abandoned. If he could reach it, they might manage to eventually reach civilization. His attacker was lying on her side. She wasn't dead, although she was incapacitated and making wheezing, choking sounds. He didn't move any closer to her. Even injured, she was still deadly—and her friend remained at large.

Elijah's gaze swept the sea of rock and boulders that encircled him.

Where is he?

Elijah had almost reached the abandoned hopper when he caught movement to his right.

The man burst out from the cover of a tor of rock, bolts of white laser searing the air. And he was coming straight for Elijah.

Throwing himself right, Elijah tumbled to the ground. Sharp rock dug into his palms once more, yet he ignored the pain.

A bolt whispered past his shoulder, its cold heat numbing his skin.

Jaw clenched, Elijah rolled sideways and returned fire, However, he was careful to keep moving, even as bolts of laser plowed into the ochre earth just inches from him. If he halted, even for an instant, one of those laser bolts would strike him.

The attack kicked up a cloud of dust, creating a hazy screen between the two of them.

Elijah bounced to his feet and continued toward the hopper.

He only had seconds before the dust cleared—he had to make the most of it.

The thud of flesh and bone colliding reached him then, followed by a pained grunt.

The dust cleared, and Elijah's gaze settled upon two figures struggling on the ground, just a few yards away: Isla and the marine.

Elijah breathed a curse. He couldn't help it—the woman's bravery impressed him.

Twice in one fight, she'd saved his neck.

However, her recklessness was going to get her killed.

"Isla!"

She ignored him. Rolling on top of the man, she smashed her fist into his throat. Her opponent choked a curse and struck upwards, punching her in the jaw. Isla's head snapped back.

Elijah holstered his weapon and closed the final distance to the idling hopper. Leaping on, he kicked the craft into life and accelerated toward the two struggling figures.

And as he drew closer, he saw Isla's opponent now had her under him. He was trying to dig his fingers into her eye sockets.

Things were about to go badly for her.

Elijah let go of the handlebar with one hand, drew his laser-pistol, and fired. He'd been aiming for the man's head but caught his shoulder instead. Isla had just driven her knee into the man's groin, causing him to lurch upward.

The shot knocked him off Isla.

Not wasting a moment, she rolled to her feet and raced over to where Elijah sat astride the hopper. She then leaped on behind him.

"Get us out of here!" she gasped.

Elijah was about to turn the hopper around when he spied movement to his right.

Clutching his injured shoulder, and limping badly, the man he'd just shot lurched toward his own hopper, which hovered a few yards distant.

Fuck it, he was harder to bring down than a cyborg.

Elijah drew his pistol once more—and pulled the trigger.

The bolt hit the man square between the shoulder blades. Sprawling forward, he collapsed upon the dusty ground. Elijah shifted his aim to the hopper.

Surely, the bastard wouldn't get up again? However, if he did, he'd be chasing them on foot.

A stream of laser bolts hit the craft.

The hopper flew into the air before crashing onto the hard earth, its sleek frame cracking in half.

Holstering his pistol once more, Elijah turned the hopper west and opened the throttle. The craft leaped forward—living up to its name.

They hurtled toward the mountains, dust billowing in their wake.

It was only when they reached the foothills, at least five klicks distant from where they'd been attacked, that Elijah slowed the hopper.

Bringing it to a smooth halt, he lowered the craft to the ground and then cut the engine.

In the aftermath of the attack, his pulse was still racing, and his breathing hadn't returned to normal.

That had been close.

He couldn't believe he was still alive—or that the woman seated behind him was partially responsible for it.

Isla had held on to his waist while they'd been traveling, yet she let go now.

Elijah shook his head in rueful disbelief before throwing a leg over the front of the hopper and sliding to the ground.

He supposed he should thank her.

However, when he turned to his companion, he found himself staring into the barrel of a laser-pistol.

His laser-pistol.

She'd helped herself to it as he'd pulled up without him even noticing.

Elijah froze, disbelief rippling through him.

Not again.

Isla stepped forward, lowering the weapon slightly so that it no longer pointed at his head, but at his heart. Her face was hard, her dark-blue eyes narrowed.

"So, this is it then," he murmured.

"Yes."

His mouth twisted. "I don't understand. Why bother saving my hide back there if you're going to shoot me now?"

She flashed him a tight smile. "I didn't come all this way to let someone *else* kill you, Mir-Ferrin."

Elijah drew in a slow, deep breath—and then a strange calm descended upon him. "Is this what your daughter would want?"

A muscle flickered on her jaw. "Don't fuck with me. I know what you're doing."

"And what's that?"

He had to keep her talking.

While she was engaged with him, she was less likely to shoot him. He needed to buy himself time.

"You're trying to make me feel guilty … so I'll second-guess myself." She stepped forward, shifting so they were standing close, so that the barrel of the laser-pistol was pressed against his left pectoral muscle. "You're trying to trick me."

"No," he replied softly. "I'm merely pointing out that you're so deep in this … so obsessed by a desire to get even … that you can't see reality anymore." He broke off then, swallowing hard. It was difficult to keep calm with the feel of hot metal biting into his skin. "The truth is, you shouldn't even be here, Isla … but hunting me was easier than facing your grief, wasn't it?"

"Don't talk as if you know me," she growled. Isla's face was all taut angles now. Her eyes glittered. "You know *nothing* about what I've been through."

Nausea rolled over Elijah. *Shit.* Instead of talking her down, he was just making things worse. "You're right," he answered huskily. "I don't know you … but I don't want to be your enemy." He broke off there, sucking in a steadying breath before continuing. "Put the gun away, Isla. Let's start again. You're no longer my captive, and I'm no longer your target. Let's work together, so we can both get off this planet alive … so we can *both* go home."

Isla's finger flexed on the trigger.

Gods, she wanted him to stop talking. He wouldn't wriggle out of this.

Pull the trigger. The voice was screaming in her head, yet she couldn't seem to comply. It was as if her finger were frozen.

Drawing in a deep breath, Isla thought of Cathal then. If she let the memories of her husband flood over her, if she recalled the fear, the desperation, she'd seen in his eyes on the day he'd died, she'd find the strength she needed to kill this bastard.

But, try as she might, she couldn't seem to recall the exact lines and details of her husband's face or the cadence of his voice. Dammit, only three years had passed. Everything should be as sharp as if he'd died just a couple of days earlier.

Yet it wasn't.

And suddenly, the pointlessness of it all hit Isla. The realization shocked her, as if she'd just taken a stun bolt to the chest.

Cathal was dead and gone. Her quest for revenge meant nothing to anyone but her.

His sister had grieved him but had been able to move forward. And even Bea, who'd adored her father, didn't carry his loss upon her back the way Isla did. Isla had nursed this wound, planned for the day she'd take her reckoning. But now it was within her grasp, now that all she had to do was pull the trigger and claim it, the whole enterprise felt empty.

When Mir-Ferrin had pointed out, on their first night in the survival-dome, that killing him wouldn't bring her husband back, she'd felt like spitting at him. Of course, it wouldn't. However, it would give her the closure she so desperately sought.

Only now, Isla realized there could be no closure.

Truth was, Mir-Ferrin was right. She'd never truly grieved her husband. After the initial shock at losing him, she'd walled up that part of her and instead focused on her rage. She'd been so fixated on it that she'd walked away from her daughter without a backward glance.

Isla's throat constricted. "Curse you," she whispered, her voice catching. "Curse us both."

She stepped back then, taking the laser-pistol with her.

The clan-lord blinked. His tanned face was slick with sweat, his pupils dilated.

Swallowing hard, to try and dislodge the tightness in her throat that threatened to choke her, Isla clicked the laser-pistol energy setting to zero with her thumb and tossed the weapon away.

It landed in the dirt a few yards distant.

Isla then swiveled on her heel and stalked off, leaving Mir-Ferrin staring after her.

Elijah watched Isla stride away.

His heart kicked hard against his ribs as the adrenalin subsided.

Despite that he'd done his best to talk Isla down, he'd been so sure it was over for him—but she hadn't pulled the trigger. Somehow, he'd gotten through to her.

Even so, he'd been shocked when she stepped back and tossed the pistol aside.

Walking over to the discarded weapon, he retrieved it. Wordlessly, he then holstered the gun and turned back to Isla.

She stopped a few yards distant, her back to him. Her slender body was rigid—even from this distance, he could feel the fury vibrating off her.

Anger at him. At herself. After all, she'd put everything on the line for this mission, and she'd had him at her mercy. And yet she had spared his life. She was likely regretting throwing the pistol away—which is why he'd picked it up.

Elijah didn't make the mistake of approaching her or speaking to her. Isla was a primed pyro-grenade right now.

Moving across to the parked hopper, he lowered himself onto its seat and waited.

The minutes stretched out before Isla swiveled on her heel and marched back to him.

Her face was set, her blue eyes shuttered, as she drew up in front of Elijah and folded her arms across her chest.

He met her gaze, careful to keep his own expression neutral. This was a turning point in their relationship, and he didn't want to provoke her. "Can we start over then?" he asked cautiously.

Her gaze flicked down to the holstered pistol on his thigh. "Did you mean what you said about not taking me captive again?"

He nodded. "When we arrive at Scull Basin, you're free to go your own way."

It still surprised him he'd promised her that—although she'd had him by the balls at the time.

There went his leverage against the Mir-Brennans. Nonetheless, he'd not go back on his word.

Isla's attention returned to his face, distrust flickering in her eyes. However, after a long pause, she nodded. "All right then," she murmured. "Let's go."

13. JUST LIKE THAT

COMMANDER NIX AWOKE to pain. Agony burned across his chest, back, and left shoulder. However, the pain meant he was alive.

Groaning, he rolled over onto his back, his eyes flickering open.

A yellow-tinged overcast sky hung overhead.

Nix's mouth twisted. He'd hoped to be off this shitty planet quickly, but his stay on Estradia was going to be longer than planned.

Rolling onto his right side, Nix clenched his jaw against the fire that burned in his wounds and pushed himself up.

The laser bolts had torn into his body armor and burned the skin underneath. But despite the pain, the wounds were relatively superficial. Some antiseptic and plasti-skin would start the healing process.

Nix's gaze shifted over to the prone figure lying a few yards away.

Lieutenant Rena, however, wasn't so fortunate.

Pushing himself off the ground, he staggered over to her.

As he drew close, he realized there was no point in checking her vitals. His lieutenant lay on her side, facing him, yet her eyes were sightless, her face slack. Dark blood pooled around her; already, it was congealing. A cloud of midges had settled over her, but they lifted as he approached.

Nix stopped before Rena and gazed down at her.

He then whispered a curse. Rena had been one of his best.

Nix hunkered down and swiped his bloodied fingers over her eyelids, closing them.

Sitting back on his heels, he scowled. Elijah Mir-Ferrin should have been an easy enough mark: on foot and not wearing any protective clothing.

Nonetheless, he had a lethal aim with a laser-pistol and handled himself well in a fight. And that mystery woman—who'd been freed from her restraints—fought like an assassin.

Nix cast a glance over his shoulder at the wreck of his hopper, and heat ignited in his stomach.

The clan-lord had destroyed his only means of catching up with him.

A beeping intruded then, and the commander glanced down at his wrist-comm.

A chill washed over him, dousing the fire in his gut.

Lucas Mir-Ferrin was calling.

They came upon Scull Basin suddenly. Elijah had just crested a hill, but he slowed the hopper at the sight of a spiky carpet of dun-colored stone buildings spreading out below him.

"I don't believe it," Isla murmured behind him. "You *do* have a sense of direction, after all."

Elijah snorted. He'd been sure that this settlement lay to the west. However, he had misjudged how long it would take to reach it. Dusk was on the verge of setting, and after three long, exhausting days of trekking across the wasteland, there was nothing sweeter than seeing civilization again.

"Just in time too," he replied, glancing down at the warning light on the dashboard. It had been glowing red for the last twenty minutes. "We're almost out of charge."

A pause followed before Isla asked, "Where are you dropping me off?" Her tone was light, yet there was a wary edge to it. They hadn't spoken during the journey since climbing onboard the hopper again.

She didn't trust his word—yet Elijah didn't take offense.

He didn't trust her either.

"Not sure yet … somewhere in the center." He paused then. "I'll need to find a place to stay the night … and get something to eat. We'll *both* need credits though. Once we stop, I'll check the hopper's storage locker and see if we're carrying a PCSD." He paused then. "Of course, if it's password access only, it'll be no good to us."

"Well, in that case, you'll have to sell the hopper."

Elijah frowned. He didn't like that suggestion much; he needed the craft to reach the capital. This afternoon's hopper journey had given him time to think, to come up with a plan. Right now, what he required was an ally, one with resources.

If he could get his hands on a high-security Mir-Ferrin wrist-comm, like his old one, he could contact Commander Grav. Out of all those who served him, Elijah trusted Grav the most. However, even if he got hold of a standard issue comm, it wouldn't have the access and encryption he needed to locate and contact *Conqueror*, Grav's ship.

Instead, he'd look for help closer to hand. The planet's governor resided in Crelcaster, and Elijah had to get him onside. The city also had a spaceport—their only way off this desolate planet. There weren't any other spaceports on Estradia; the minerals mined here had to be shipped to the capital via trans-barge.

He slowed the craft further still then, his gaze sweeping the basin nestling under the shadow of a great oche peak that pierced the darkening sky.

Scull Basin blended in with its surroundings so well that, at first, he hadn't seen it—only the satellite dishes and antennae bristling from the cone-like dwellings gave it away. Built of local stone, the buildings, which resembled large stalagmites, thrust out of the jaundiced earth.

Elijah released the throttle and skimmed down the rocky hillside toward town. As he approached the tallest of the cones, he spied figures clad in loose jumpsuits filing out of an entrance way. He guessed this was one of the many mineral refineries that studded Estradia. The workers glanced their way as the hopper sped by.

Behind him, Elijah felt Isla tense. She didn't like being observed either. Better that they kept as low a profile as possible—for it wasn't improbable that his brother had more assassins out looking for him.

The main gate into town was unguarded. Yet they drew more stares as Elijah slowed down and navigated the grid of dusty gullies between the buildings in search of accommodation.

Elijah glanced around, taking in his surroundings. Scull Basin was busier than he'd expected. At this hour, several citizens were out, shopping after finishing work for the day. There was a surprising amount of traffic too; hoppers streaked by while some locals preferred to ride upon large, sleek lizards that crawled down the streets, their long bodies moving from side to side.

Above the bustle, the tall, spiky buildings cast long shadows. The air was cooling rapidly now.

Elijah's skin prickled as suspicious looks continued to track them. "I don't like the attention we're attracting," he muttered.

"Neither do I," Isla replied. "Best you drop me off … and we both do our best to disappear."

Elijah pulled up at a charging station and dismounted from the hopper. He then shackled it to one of the chargers.

"So … do we have credits?" Isla asked. She too had climbed off the hopper and was brushing dust off her clothing. Like him, her clothing was sweat-stained and filthy. Bruised, scratched, and bloodied—neither of them looked reputable. Was it any wonder they'd drawn stares on the way in?

"Let's see," Elijah answered, opening one of the storage lockers on the side of the hopper. In amongst a survival-dome and a first-aid kit, he found a small circular device: a Portable Currency Storage Device. He then illuminated the display on the top of the PCSD and grunted. "We're in luck … it's military-standard-issue, which means they don't password it … makes it easier to pass between teams."

Isla's sigh of relief was audible. "How much do we have?"

"There are around two hundred hard credits on this … it won't get either of us far." He met Isla's eye then, his grip tightening on the PCSD. His mouth quirked. "And since I'm the man with the money, it looks like you're going to have to stick with me a while longer."

Isla's brows drew together. "Excuse me?"

"Well, it's too late in the day to find a bank, buy you an empty PCSD, and transfer funds."

Her nostrils flared. "I'd rather we went our separate ways tonight."

Elijah raised his eyebrows. "You won't get far without any credits."

A muscle in Isla's jaw flexed, her blue eyes narrowing. "We'll see about that."

Then, to his surprise, she swiveled on her heel and stalked away.

Elijah watched her go. He couldn't believe it—it seemed too easy. No farewells. No parting insults.

Just like that, Isla Mir-Brennan walked out of his life.

"Arrogant shit," Isla muttered as she marched into the first guesthouse she encountered—a squat clay cone with a glowing sign above the entrance advertising 'cheap rooms'. "*Since I'm the man with the money*." She should have told him where he could stick the PCSD. Better yet, she should have punched him in the mouth and stolen the device.

It was true—Isla wouldn't get far without money. But she'd rather scrub floors in a pleasure house for the next month than let that bastard get the upper hand again. Pride had also prevented her from grabbing the survival-dome before stalking off—something she hoped she wouldn't regret later.

Just find somewhere to stay tonight, and tomorrow, you'll steal a hopper and funds, if you have to, she counseled herself. *You're a survivor, you'll figure something out when you're rested.*

However, the human female who ran this guesthouse wasn't interested in renting out a room to someone for free, even when Isla offered to work in the kitchen to earn her keep.

Undefeated, Isla left the establishment and moved on to the next one.

An hour later, as the last of the light faded from Estradia's moody sky, and its twin moons rose, she was no longer so confident.

Apart from one innkeeper, who'd suggested she 'service' him and any interested patrons, Isla hadn't found anyone willing to give her shelter for the night.

It was now bitterly cold outdoors, and she was shivering in her light jumpsuit. The streets were largely deserted, apart from the odd hopper that sped past in a streak of light.

Only Isla was foolish enough to be wandering the canyon-like streets of Scull Basin. She was seriously starting to regret not taking that dome now. She could have pitched it in a back alley somewhere.

Drawing up before a tall, thin stalagmite-shaped building, she halted a moment, steeling herself for the degrading experience that would likely lie within. Some of the buildings in Scull Basin were made of mudbrick, yet this one had a smooth, clay façade and tiny oval windows. Light glowed from the portals, a welcoming sight indeed, and the aroma of cooking smells wafted out onto the street. Isla's belly growled in response.

A flickering sign hung over the cave-like doorway: *Rosa's Inn.*

"Right, Rosa," Isla murmured. "Let's see if you need a dishwasher."

She made her way inside, halting as the door slid shut behind her. Surveying the interior, Isla frowned. Suddenly, she wished she'd kept that laser-pistol. Tossing it away so Mir-Ferrin could retrieve it had been a mistake. She'd feel more comfortable venturing into these places with one strapped to her thigh.

Dimly lit and lined with shadowy alcoves, the air thick with clove smoke, the tavern had a seedy look. Most of the alcoves were occupied this evening—humans, Vulkar, Gibbits, and Rendak clad in dusty jumpsuits reclined at tables. Like most locals she'd seen since arriving at Scull Basin, they likely all worked at the mineral refinery. Stares swiveled Isla's way, raking over her.

A female Lebbin moved across the floor toward Isla, wending her way between tables, her long tail flicking from side to side. She ducked her slender head, bulbous eyes regarding her with interest. "Good evening," she greeted Isla, her voice high and melodious. "What can I get you?"

"I need a room for the night … and a meal."

The Lebbin's head bobbed. "I can provide you with both." She then turned, limbs flailing. "This way."

"Wait," Isla said before clearing her throat. "I don't have any credits."

The innkeeper halted, turning her way. "Excuse me?"

Isla favored her with a hasty, contrite smile. She was exhausted and thirsty, and so hungry that the tantalizing aromas drifting out of the nearby kitchen were making it hard to concentrate.

"I'm a hard worker," she said, holding the Lebbin's gaze. "I'll wash dishes and even scrub floors if I need to … just one night's accommodation and a meal. That's all I'm asking." She heaved in a deep breath before exhaling slowly. "Please."

The innkeeper regarded her for a long moment before giving an elegant shrug. "I'm sorry, but no credits … no room."

Isla's shoulders slumped. She could still feel gazes upon her; half the common room was likely listening to this exchange, yet she didn't care.

She didn't want to move on to another tavern.

And yet she didn't want to beg either.

Desperation and pride fought before the latter bested the former. Throat constricting, she nodded and turned away.

"It's all right … she can share *my* room."

The male voice—all too familiar—was tinged with irritation.

Drawing in a deep breath, Isla swiveled, her gaze locking with Elijah Mir-Ferrin's.

The clan-lord was seated in a small booth a few feet away. His clothing was clean, and his hair was damp, as if he'd recently taken a shower. "And I might as well buy her a meal too."

Isla's pulse quickened, her skin prickling with humiliation. Dammit, she hadn't seen him on her way in. He'd heard the whole conversation and knew just how hopeless her situation was.

"This isn't a pleasure house," the Lebbin informed him, her tone cooling. "You can't—"

"It's okay," Isla cut her off. With that, she crossed to the booth and slid into the seat opposite the man she'd hoped never to see again. "I know him."

14. YOU'RE WELCOME

ISLA DIDN'T KNOW what was in the stew Rosa served up—but she didn't care. It was the best thing she'd ever tasted.

She'd been tense as she waited for her meal to arrive, refusing to talk to Mir-Ferrin or meet his eye; but at the smell of the rich stew many of the patrons were consuming, her mouth filled with saliva. Suddenly, she'd been too hungry to care about anything except filling her belly.

Hunched over the bowl Rosa had slid before her, Isla spooned stew into her mouth. Despite that she wanted to inhale the food, she forced herself to eat slowly, to savor it.

She didn't want her stomach to rebel, for apart from the odd nutri-bar over the past days, she'd eaten very little.

Likewise, Mir-Ferrin ate with slow deliberation. A basket of fresh bread sat between them, which they also steadily ate their way through.

Eventually, as she wiped up the last of her stew with a scrap of bread, Isla released a deep sigh.

Mir-Ferrin's mouth lifted at the corners as he raised his cup to his lips and took a sip. "A simple 'thank you' will suffice."

Isla remained mutinously silent.

He shrugged. "If you recall, I offered to put you up tonight ... you didn't need to exhaust yourself trailing around to every lodging in town."

Isla cleared her throat. "About this room you've rented—"

"Don't worry," he cut her off. "There's only one bed ... but I'll sleep on the floor."

She cocked an eyebrow. "Considerate of you."

"It is ... and don't worry, you're welcome."

Silence settled between them once more. Isla's supper churned uneasily in her stomach. His presence put her on edge—it was a reminder that this man always seemed to get the best of her.

She hated that.

Rosa neared then, wiping down the bar top with one of her hands, while she cleared their empty dishes with two others. "Where have you traveled from?" she asked, her gaze flicking from Mir-Ferrin to Isla.

"We had some mechanical trouble with our ship and had to make a forced landing around three days' walk east of here," the clan-lord replied.

The Lebbin's eyes widened. "Were you on that battlecruiser that was destroyed in Estradia's orbit?"

Mir-Ferrin shook his head, his expression shuttering. He leaned forward then, his gaze fusing with Rosa's. "I need to get to Crelcaster. How far is it from here?"

The Lebbin inclined her head. "It depends on how you're traveling … there aren't any shunts on Estradia, but trans-barges carrying ore leave most mornings. They take passengers, although they're slow, as they stop at two towns en route. It's a two-day journey."

"I've got a hopper," Mir-Ferrin answered. "A fast one."

"Then you could get there in a day … if you leave as soon as dawn breaks." Rosa paused, her brow furrowing. "I'd be careful in the capital if I were you. There's been more rioting over the past couple of days. The streets aren't safe."

Isla's mouth pursed. "The citizens object to Mir-Ferrin rule then?"

"It's not that," Rosa replied, cutting her a bemused look. "There's been trouble between religious extremists and the locals."

Mir-Ferrin frowned. "The Followers of Wis?"

Rosa nodded.

"But they're usually peaceful," Isla pointed out.

"They are … but there's a faction of extremists who have turned militant," the innkeeper answered. "They call themselves *The Creed of Truth* ... and they've dedicated themselves to ridding this sector of 'impurity'."

Isla snorted. "Well then, they've started in the right territory."

Once again, the innkeeper favored her with a puzzled glance. She then departed to deliver drinks to a rowdy group of human males at one of the booths on the other side of the common room.

When they were alone, Mir-Ferrin met Isla's eye. "Look ... why don't you come with me to Crelcaster?"

Isla frowned. "Really?" she asked, not bothering to hide her suspicion.

He huffed a sigh. "Don't get me wrong ... I'm just as keen as you are to part ways ... but since the hopper takes two passengers, the offer's there."

Isla's mouth pursed. She *did* need to get to the capital. Apparently, Estradia's only spaceport was located at Crelcaster, and although Isla didn't yet know how she was going to get off this planet, heading for the spaceport seemed like a good start.

It was one step closer to being reunited with Bea.

Sure, she could steal her own hopper tomorrow, but then she'd have the local garrison on her back. She wasn't any use to her daughter locked up in a detention cell for theft.

Swallowing the last of her pride, she nodded.

The clan-lord leaned back in his seat and watched her over the rim of his cup. "There's no Mir-Brennan embassy on this planet," he said after a pause. "But if you stick with me for a bit, once I see the governor, I can organize your passage off-world."

Isla stilled. She didn't understand this man at all. "Why would you do that?"

Mir-Ferrin favored her with a rare smile. "I'm not sure."

They finished their drinks in silence, while the hum and babble of galactic tongues rose and fell around them.

Rosa and her two server-droid assistants were kept busy, and after a while, a group of Crall took up position at the end of the bar and started playing flutes.

The haunting melody floated through the common room.

The music was soothing, and Isla started to relax. She watched the musicians, noting how nimbly their long fingers moved over their flutes. The air inside the inn was stifling and overly warm. The sweet scent of clove smoke had grown even heavier as two more patrons lit pipes farther down the bar. The smoke stung Isla's eyes and tickled the back of her throat; it was also making her feel a little lightheaded. She was close to dozing off here.

Eventually, Mir-Ferrin stifled a yawn. "Come on … we've got an early start tomorrow."

Nodding, Isla slid out of the booth, waiting while he did the same. She then followed him from the smoky, overly warm, common room and climbed the spiral stairwell.

Mir-Ferrin led her to a room on the top floor of the inn. Crammed into the attic space, with a small cell-like window too high to look out of, it was claustrophobically narrow. Isla didn't care though. After days of sleeping in a cramped survival-dome, this room was luxury.

"Looks cozy," she said eyeing the single bed up against the wall. She then turned to her companion. This room seemed even smaller with the clan-lord in it. Their gazes met, before she flashed him a rueful look. "Although the floor looks uncomfortable."

Mir-Ferrin shrugged and moved to the closet in the corner. Opening it, he retrieved a quilt and a blanket. "It'll do."

Heaving a sigh, Isla glanced over at the door leading into the bathroom. Mir-Ferrin told her earlier there was plenty of hot water, a washer and drier, and clean robes to wear while they laundered their clothing.

Her nose wrinkled then. Just as well, for she could smell herself now—and the odor wasn't pleasant.

"Do you want to use the bathroom first?" she asked, remembering her manners.

Mir-Ferrin shook his head. "I already did earlier. You go ahead."

Relieved, Isla headed for the bathroom. Locking herself inside, she stripped off her clothes, stuffed them into the automatic launderer, and switched it on. She then stepped into the shower. Days of grime sloughed off her, dirty water swirling down the plughole. Isla turned her face up to the hot needles of water, her eyes fluttering shut.

Gods, she'd never enjoyed a shower so much.

Eventually, she switched off the water and stepped out of the cubicle, pink, glowing, and smelling of spicy body wash. The launderer was whirring now as it dried her clothing. Wrapping herself in one of the soft robes hanging behind the bathroom door, Isla re-entered the bedroom.

To her surprise, she found the clan-lord asleep on his makeshift mattress on the floor next to the bed. Sprawled on his back, his chest slowly rising and falling, he slung one arm high, using it as a pillow for his head.

Isla halted, her gaze traveling over him.

He was vulnerable right now—with his neck, chest, and stomach exposed. She could grab the laser-pistol still strapped to his thigh and shoot him.

But she wouldn't.

Not after her last failed attempt.

Why hadn't she been able to pull the damn trigger?

Trouble was, she'd gotten to know Elijah Mir-Ferrin a little over the past few days. He'd once been nothing more than an object of hate, something to avenge herself upon. She didn't like the clan-lord any more than she had initially—yet she now saw him as a real person.

Mir-Ferrin's face had softened in sleep. His relaxed features highlighted his chiseled bone structure: high cheekbones, aristocratic nose, and sensual mouth. His eyelashes were long and dark, lying against the tanned skin of his cheeks.

She wasn't blind; there was no denying the man was attractive.

Isla drew in a deep, steadying breath.

All those months of training, and you let him get to you, she berated herself, bitterness tightening her chest. *That isn't the Galbreth way.*

15. ONLY THE STRONG SURVIVE

SHOVING ASIDE SELF-LOATHING, Isla stepped over Mir-Ferrin's prone form and, still wearing her robe, climbed onto the bed, wriggling under the covers.

She rolled onto her side then, observing the clan-lord's sleeping face.

And as she watched him, he stirred—those sinfully long lashes fluttering open. His dark eyes, so dark-brown they were almost black, fastened upon her. "You took your time in there," he observed, his voice husky with sleep. "I dropped off."

"Good for you." She switched off the glow-lamp next to the bed and twisted over onto her back. It was dark inside the room now, almost oppressively so.

Silence settled, and Isla's eyelids were growing heavy when the clan-lord's voice roused her. "Can we go over our plan for tomorrow?"

Groggily, she glanced over at Mir-Ferrin. However, it was so dark she could only see his silhouette. "You have one then?"

He gave a soft snort. "We need to be out of here as early as we can … my brother's likely to make a stop here tomorrow."

Despite that Isla knew he couldn't see her, she pulled a face. "You're a dangerous man to travel with."

"Well, you're welcome to stay behind here," he replied, "and find your own way off-planet."

Isla pursed her lips. They both knew she'd actually prefer that option, if only she had the funds. "Will the hopper be fully charged by morning?" she asked, deliberately changing the subject.

"Yes, although I'll have to recharge it at least once en route. Rosa assures us that there are two stops so that shouldn't be a problem."

"And you know where to find the governor?"

"I checked the nav-system on the hopper earlier. His mansion is within easy reach of the center."

"It sounds as if you've got most things covered then." Isla paused, her brow furrowing. "But are you sure the governor will help you?"

"No ... I've only spoken with him once and didn't warm to him especially. I'll remind him that since I didn't go down with *Defiance*, I'm still clan-lord." He paused then. "Before you turned up earlier, Rosa had the latest news-reel screening above the bar. My brother isn't wasting his time making grief-stricken speeches it seems. He's already asserting his dominance ... and calling for support from his governors."

"You can't be surprised by that," she replied.

"I'm not ... but I may need to *bribe* Yannic Mir-Ferrin into being cooperative."

"With what exactly?"

"With promises. Yannic Mir-Ferrin is going to have to make a choice ... loyalty to me or Lucas. I just have to ensure my deal is sweeter."

Isla made a disgusted sound in the back of her throat. "You really are a sly bunch of bastards," she muttered. "Growing up in your household must have been fun."

He huffed a humorless laugh. "Believe me, it wasn't." Another pause followed then. "There were times, when I was kid, when I was sure I must have been adopted."

Isla snorted a laugh. "Why would you think that?"

"You think I'm like the rest of them," he replied, "but I'm not. I can act the part, but I never fit in." His voice hardened then. "That doesn't mean I can't rule better than any of them though ... I see things my father never did."

Isla digested these words. She was tempted to sneer, to tell him he did a pretty good job at living up to his family's reputation—but that would be a lie. Despite everything, she'd noticed that he *was* different. There was a thoughtful, measured edge to him that she hadn't noticed in Mican or Tian Mir-Ferrin.

He'd had plenty of opportunities to reveal a cruel or petty side over the past days, yet—apart from a bit of snarling when she tried to kill him—he hadn't. If she was honest, he surprised her.

Of course, his life was in ruins. Just days earlier, he'd ruled his clan, had been in control of his life, been supremely secure. Now, everyone except his brother thought he was dead. And Lucas was hunting him.

Right now, Elijah Mir-Ferrin must be questioning who he was and what he stood for. This whole experience would be humiliating.

"I spent some time with Tian," she admitted after a pause. That wasn't surprising. After all, the youngest Mir-Ferrin brother had married Jenna and lived at Mir-Brennan Tower for a couple of years. "Cathal wanted to trust him, but I never did. He could be charming … and he knew how to get his way … yet he could never hide the calculation in his eyes."

"That was Tian. He was incensed when father told him he'd have to marry Jenna Mir-Brennan … he never realized it was a backhanded compliment." Elijah paused. "I always thought him the most devious of my brothers, but he wasn't."

"So, you weren't close to either of them?"

"No. We were brought up to be rivals, not friends."

Silence fell then, the seconds sliding by until Isla sighed. "I wasn't raised in an easy environment either … although it wasn't as cut-throat as yours," she murmured, surprised that she felt compelled to share her past with this man. "My parents were never demonstrative … it isn't the Galbreth way. We're supposed to come out of the womb fighting."

The clan-lord gave a soft laugh. "So, I've heard."

"*Fight or die, Isla!*" she said, mimicking her father's booming voice. "Father made sure I never forgot it." That wasn't an exaggeration. Isla couldn't recall her father ever telling her he loved her. Not that she'd ever admit such to Mir-Ferrin. Their conversation had already become too personal for her liking.

"No wonder you're tough, Isla," Mir-Ferrin murmured after a lengthy pause. "You've been on guard your whole life, haven't you?"

Isla's throat tightened. "I changed after I married Cathal," she replied, her tone cooling. "He made me feel safe … he softened me." She broke off there, her pulse accelerating. "But then your family took him from me, and I realized my father was right all along." She sucked in a deep breath before concluding, "Life is harsh, and the Gods are pitiless, Mir-Ferrin … only the strong survive."

As planned, they left Scull Basin early.

The sun had barely started to lighten the eastern sky, and had yet to clear the huge peak that loomed over the town, when Elijah angled the hopper toward the north gate.

The network of narrow ravines that made up Scull Basin was deserted at this hour, for a shadow still lay over the town. The night's deep chill hadn't entirely lifted, and the skin of Elijah's bare arms prickled as he crouched over the hand-bars.

It was possibly still a little too early, but he didn't want to take any chances.

He'd been exhausted the night before, yet worries over what his brother might do had ensured he slept fitfully. Eventually, he'd awoken an hour before he needed to, and had lain there, staring up at the darkness, listening to the soft, rhythmic sound of Isla's breathing. Their conversation the night before had taken him aback. He hadn't expected to find himself so at ease with her, or for her to speak so candidly with him.

Their relationship had shifted in the past day—and they both saw each other differently, it seemed.

And as he'd stared up at the shadowed ceiling, it had hit him that, apart from Aria, he'd had few frank conversations with women over the years. Despite that he put on a good front, he really wasn't that comfortable with the opposite sex.

It was an irony then that he felt so relaxed with a woman who'd tried to kill him multiple times.

Elijah's thoughts had shifted then to Lucas, and he tried to guess his brother's next move. As he'd told Isla, his brother would know that his minions had failed to kill him—and would have figured out that Scull Basin was the nearest settlement. He'd come here next.

However, Elijah wasn't focused on his brother at present. Instead, he angled the hopper toward the north gate.

They were nearly through when Isla's gasp made him glance over his shoulder.

Descending from the west, its lights blinking, was a mid-sized bronze shuttle. The craft was lowering itself onto the rocky hillside on the other side of town. The shuttle was low now, just seconds from touching down.

"Shit," he muttered. "They're here already."

Elijah's heart started to slam against his ribcage. He'd timed their departure just right, after all.

Any earlier, and the pilots might have spotted the hopper racing up the northern hillside, and any later, and Elijah might have found all the exits from Scull Basin blocked.

The hopper accelerated up the hill, wending its way through the high stacked tors that studded the dusty earth. Elijah bent low over the handlebars, concentrating on navigating the craft through the perilous terrain. He didn't chance a look over his shoulder to see if anyone was coming after him.

No doubt, Isla would warn him if that happened.

His jaw clenched then. He didn't want to be running from his brother—he wanted to face him.

And he would. He'd deal with Lucas, all right—but he wanted to be in a stronger position when he did so. Once he reached Crelcaster and gained the support of the governor, he'd take great pleasure in bringing his brother down.

Isla climbed off the hopper and removed her goggles, wiping away the thin layer of yellow dirt that now covered them. The dust on this planet got everywhere—into her hair, eyes, and nostrils. And the bitter taste of it lingered on her tongue. She wondered if the citizens of Scull Basin even enjoyed living on this rock. Surely, the rank-smelling air would get to you after a while.

She was looking forward to stepping onto a spaceship and breathing filtered air once more, and to leaving Estradia's depressing overcast skies behind her.

Stretching out her stiff limbs, for it was mid-morning and they'd been traveling since dawn, Isla watched Mir-Ferrin stride over to the small awning-covered kiosk a few yards away. They'd left Scull Basin without eating anything and had now drained the single canister of rehydration tonic they carried. The clan-lord would need to use some of those dwindling hard credits on his PCSD.

Isla watched him walk away, noting the tense set of his shoulders.

Mir-Ferrin had been taciturn and on edge ever since their departure from Scull Basin. Isla didn't blame him. The sight of that bronze shuttle had unnerved her too. She'd been sure they'd be spotted, but the Gods had been with them this morning, for they'd sped away from Scull Basin without being pursued.

They'd parked on the outskirts of a settlement—a cluster of stalagmite-shaped dwellings set around the spire of a water tower and a silver mineral silo. Like Scull Basin, this village was built out of local stone and clay, and it blended in perfectly with the landscape.

As Isla waited, a sleek large lizard appeared from between two conelike buildings. A cloaked, vaguely humanoid figure perched atop it, a deep cowl shadowing their face. Wearing a saddle and a harness, its small dark eyes darting around, the reptile crawled, with surprising speed south, away from the village.

Intrigued, Isla watched it go. She'd seen those lizards in Scull Basin and wondered if they were native to the planet.

The clan-lord returned then with a couple of canisters of tonic and two parcels. Wordlessly, he handed her one of the packages. Isla tore back the wrapping to find a slab of chargrilled meat sandwiched between two pieces of oily bread.

She took a bite, and, unbidden, a groan escaped her.

Gods, this was the best thing she'd ever tasted.

She looked up then, to find Mir-Ferrin watching her. "You like it then?"

"I do," she said, swallowing her mouthful. "It's delicious."

"It's a Ragnor ... an eight-legged insectoid," he replied casually. "Its bite is deadly, although the vendor assured me the rest of it is good eating."

Isla, who'd been about to take another large bite of her sandwich, froze. "That's not the thing that attacked us in the survival-dome, is it?"

"I assume so."

Isla's stomach clenched. She eyed the meat she'd been enjoying and tried to decide whether she cared what it was she was eating.

Bile stung the back of her throat. She did.

Meanwhile, Mir-Ferrin was devouring his meal without hesitation.

"Your brother should have finished scouring Scull Basin by now," she pointed out, irritated that he'd ruined her enjoyment of her food. She hoped to pay him the same favor one day.

The clan-lord glanced up, meeting her eye. After swallowing a mouthful, he replied, "I'm sure he will be. No doubt he'll visit *Rosa's Inn* … and once he's had a chat to the proprietor, he'll be coming after us."

"You think she'll tell him a human male matching your description stayed there … and where you're headed?"

Mir-Ferrin nodded. "She has no reason *not* to … if I'd had the credits, I'd have bought her silence."

Isla's mouth thinned. *Of course, you would have.*

She glanced about her then. Out in the wasteland, with only one laser-pistol to defend themselves, they were no match for a heavily armed shuttle.

"Well, you'd better hope Lucas is delayed," she muttered. "Or we're both dead."

16. IN PURSUIT

THE SKIN BETWEEN Elijah's shoulder blades prickled all day. He was on edge, his senses on high alert.

He kept imagining he heard the throb of powerful engines approaching. However, the roar was only the wind.

Lucas never caught up with them, and Elijah wondered why.

Maybe something had delayed him in Scull Basin.

It was almost dark by the time they finally reached the outskirts of Crelcaster. Although Elijah had opened the throttle, had pushed the hopper to its maximum speed, in bursts so as not to overheat the engines, they barely made it before nightfall.

The heavy cloud cover lifted, and the heavens turned purple, the first of the stars twinkling to life. The planet's twin golden moons were visible now, hanging so low they almost touched the horizon—while ahead, the outline of Estradia's capital bristled against the sky.

On the way in, they passed the ubiquitous mining facilities, silos, and water towers, as well as sprawling factories surrounded by security fences, before joining a busy multi-lane highway that led into the center of the city.

The suburbs sprawled for many klicks, a forest of dull-yellow clay cones. At this hour, the dwellings cast long shadows. However, there was still a lot of foot traffic about—and Elijah had to slow the hopper to avoid hitting a lizard. Like Scull Basin, many citizens here also rode reptiles. They crawled, long, sinuous bodies gleaming bronze in the fading light, through the narrow streets.

Elijah's mouth curved. *Bronze ... how fitting.* The lizards were his clan color.

He joined one of the arterial roads now, merging the craft with the flow of traffic—hoppers and trans-barges that traveled the grid that crisscrossed the capital.

Ahead, the tall, glittering, spiky buildings of the business district speared the sky. Crelcaster made Scull Basin look like a sleepy village in comparison.

They passed a temple to Wis on the way into the center—a vast crown of obsidian spires gleaming in the fading light.

Elijah frowned as his gaze slid over it. The temple was a reminder of why his flagship had been orbiting Estradia in the first place. And around two klicks away from the business district, he spied the burned-out shells of buildings and smashed-in shop fronts—evidence of the riots that had erupted in the capital with increasing frequency of late.

"How far away is the governor's residence?" Isla's breath feathered his ear.

Elijah glanced down at the dashboard in front of him and, releasing a hand from the controls, tapped the nav-display. A map of Crelcaster glowed in front of him before a red dot illuminated their location. "It's on the northern edge of the center. We should be there in around ten minutes."

"You might want to speed up a little … I don't think it's any safer to be out after dark here than anywhere else on his planet."

Elijah glanced around him. Despite the heavy flow of traffic that still streaked through the streets, the sidewalks were quickly emptying now. "Probably not," he agreed. "But we should be indoors soon enough."

He exited the wide street, flanked by buildings that thrust skyward like yellowed canine teeth, and took the orbital road that circled the business district. The spires that reared up in the city center twinkled gold and silver in the dusk light. As night settled, the city had a certain harsh beauty.

The orbital road took them north, and when Elijah exited it, he checked his nav-display once more before announcing, "It's just down this street."

They were traveling through a wealthy suburb now; the residences, although constructed of yellow-brown stone and conical shaped, were large and heavily decorated, with high walls protecting them.

Slowing the hopper, Elijah peered ahead. If the nav-display was right, the governor's mansion should be straight ahead.

It was. Huge, with intricate swirls carved upon its smooth yellow walls, the mansion dwarfed the residences on either side of it. High, spike-topped walls surrounded the complex and its grounds—while an imposing, covered security gate faced the street.

Elijah slowed the hopper to a crawl and angled it into the gateway.

He'd expected to see the governor's bodyguards there. However, when two battle-droids stepped out of the shadows, their crimson eyes spearing him, his heart leaped in his throat.

"Fuck," he grunted. "Hold on!"

Isla obeyed, her arms gripping hard around his waist as he yanked the hopper left and dove back into the stream of traffic. They barely avoided a collision with a large hopper, and horns blared. However, Elijah was too intent on getting away to pay the angry rider any notice.

And as they sped down the street, the roar of powerful engines igniting behind them made Elijah's pulse kick into a run.

"What was that all about?" Isla demanded.

"Change of plan," he growled. "The governor isn't going to help us. My brother got there first."

"How do you know?"

"A governor doesn't have battle-droids."

Isla fell silent then, remaining so while Elijah dodged the traffic and took the ramp back up onto the orbital road. He then opened the throttle. To the west, the last of the daylight was fading. A great shadow was falling across the city—and they were still outdoors.

The console in front of Elijah started to blink red then. Despite that he'd managed to recharge the hopper en route, the battery was almost drained now. Elijah muttered another curse under his breath. *Great.* Some plan he'd worked out.

Meanwhile, the roar of engines behind them warned that they hadn't lost their pursuers.

Elijah chanced a look over his shoulder and caught sight of two large black and bronze hoppers, with battle-droids crouched over the handlebars, bearing down on them.

His already racing heart started to thunder in his ears. He couldn't outrun them on the orbital road. The best they could hope for was to lose them in the suburbs.

Veering right, and cutting in front of a trans-barge, Elijah took the next exit.

This one took them into a shopping district. At this hour, the streets were empty and the shutters closed for the day. Smooth-sided clay buildings rose around them, blocking out the dark sky.

Elijah whipped the hopper into a network of labyrinthine alleyways. The light on the dashboard was blinking frantically now. He was pushing the craft to its limits—the battery wouldn't last much longer. They whizzed past glowing signs, forbidding hopper access in this area, yet Elijah ignored them.

The battle-droids were on much more powerful hoppers, but they weren't as nimble as the one they were fleeing on. Their only hope was to lose them in here.

Isla didn't utter a word as he swerved around tight corners. However, her hold on his waist tightened.

He didn't dare glance behind him again. It was hard to tell how close their pursuers were, for the roar of their engines echoed in the narrow, gully-like streets.

"They're falling back," Isla shouted then, struggling to be heard over the whine of the hopper's engine.

Seconds later, they burst out of the tangle of alleys and crossed a wide, empty plaza. A large commercial hub loomed before Elijah and Isla now—a ring of pointy cones squashed together with an arched entranceway leading into it.

Like the streets behind them, the hub was limited to pedestrians only.

But Elijah ignored these glowing signs as well. Instead, he aimed the hopper for the archway.

The heavy steel shutter was closing, three-quarters of the way down now, and Elijah heaved his weight left, bringing his passenger with him. Isla gasped a curse, her hold on him so tight now it hurt. The hopper listed and bounced off the ground, its engine screaming in protest. They slid under the shutter on their side, metal sparking against stone.

As soon as they were clear, Elijah threw himself in the opposite direction, righting the craft and bringing it to an uneven halt—just short of colliding with a shop front.

Breathing hard, he glanced around.

A large, smooth-sided tunnel, lined with shops, stretched before them. And since the hub had closed for the day, there was no one about except for utility-droids. The squat robots, with brushes rotating under them, ignored the intruders as they trundled about sweeping and washing the floor.

A heavy metallic clang sounded behind the idling hopper, followed by the clunk of locks engaging. Glancing over his shoulder, Elijah was relieved to see that the shutter had sealed. Beyond it, he could hear the muffled roar of approaching engines.

However, there was no way into the hub now.

Elijah's breathing stilled, waiting as their pursuers drew closer. The noise grew louder still before the battle-droids roared past. It was only when the sounds retreated into the distance that he slowly exhaled.

Jidea be praised. They'd been far enough ahead to get into the hub before the battle-droids entered the plaza. They hadn't seen them.

"There will be security cams in here," Isla pointed out huskily, relaxing her death-grip on his waist. "We need to get out of sight before someone spots us."

Elijah's mouth thinned. She wouldn't get any argument out of him on that.

The battery level on the console was at 'critical' now. He'd guess they had no more than a couple of minutes of juice left.

They traveled up the tunnel a short distance until they reached a narrow side-passage. Turning the hopper into it, Elijah spied a grill at the far end. It was covering the entrance to a service shaft. His mouth quirked then, an idea sparking.

Drawing the hopper to a halt, he lowered it to the ground and cut the engines. Yanking off his goggles, he dismounted and opened the storage locker at the back of the craft, retrieving a screwdriver.

Isla didn't comment as he went to the grill, hunkered down, and pried it off the wall. Elijah glanced over his shoulder then, meeting his companion's eye for the first time in hours.

Isla had also removed her googles and was still seated upon the parked hopper. Arms folded across her chest, she watched him, her expression veiled. Nonetheless, her gaze was the warmest he'd ever seen it.

Elijah cocked an eyebrow. "What do you think of our hiding place?"

"Not bad, Mir-Ferrin." She paused then, a rueful smile playing on her lips. "By the way, that was some impressive maneuvering back there."

There wasn't much space in the service shaft. Nonetheless, they just managed to fit the hopper, and themselves, inside before yanking the grill into place after them. The stone floor would make an uncomfortable bed for the night, so Isla pulled out the survival-dome. She then managed to half inflate it; the dome made a squishy mattress, but it would do.

It was dark in here, but they'd found a small glow-lamp inside the storage locker. Once switched on, it cast a soft silver light over the interior of the shaft, highlighting dull-grey paneling. The shaft stretched for a few meters in both directions before curving.

Pulling off her boots, Isla wriggled over to the far wall, leaning her back against cool metal while the clan-lord rummaged around in the hopper's locker for food. There was only one nutri-bar left, which they shared.

Legs crossed in front of her, Isla ate her meager supper slowly. It seemed like a long while since her last meal—she was glad now she'd managed to choke that Ragnor meat down in the end—and she was ravenous.

Mir-Ferrin kicked off his own boots and sat down nearby. He'd gone silent, and his gaze was unfocused as he ate; Isla imagined he was brooding about his brother.

"So," she said eventually. "I suppose we're out of allies now?"

The clan-lord swallowed his last mouthful of nutri-bar and nodded. "I should have guessed why Lucas didn't come after us today," he muttered, scowling. "Instead, he decided to go ahead to Crelcaster and wait for me there."

Isla shrugged. "Well, you've evaded him … again."

"Yeah … for the moment."

Their gazes met and held.

Isla broke eye contact first. "Let's press our advantage then," she said briskly. "I suggest we head to the spaceport first thing tomorrow and try to beg, borrow, or steal our way off Estradia."

"Are you sure you want to stick with me, Isla?" She glanced Mir-Ferrin's way once more to see he was still watching her. "As you pointed out yesterday, you'd be safer on your own."

The uncertainty on his face was surprising; it struck her then that Elijah Mir-Ferrin was actually concerned about her. The realization was disconcerting.

Pretending not to notice, she reached for the single canister of rehydration tonic that sat between them. "I would," she agreed. "But right now, we're better off together."

17. UNFORGETTABLE

LYING NEXT TO Mir-Ferrin on their makeshift mattress, Isla stared up at the riveted metal ceiling above her.

Despite that they'd escaped the battle-droids and found a safe place to shelter overnight, she was on edge. Her stomach rumbled, reminding her that half a nutri-bar wasn't nearly enough.

However, hunger wasn't the reason she was tense.

She'd hoped to sleep in a proper bed tonight—in a different room to this man. Instead, here they were, sleeping so close their elbows were almost brushing. In many ways, it had been easier keeping company with the clan-lord when she was his prisoner.

Their relationship was clear then.

He was right—with his brother after him, she'd be safer once she struck out on her own. But as much as she might want to deny it, they did work well together. And she had been impressed by how he'd handled their hopper earlier—he'd navigated that tangled web of streets with breathless precision and left their pursuers in the dust. And then that move he'd made, sliding them under the shutter just as it was closing, was brilliant.

Damn him, despite that she couldn't get off the planet without the man, he was really growing on her.

Isla clenched her jaw. She didn't want to be impressed by him. She didn't want to *like* him.

"You seem unsettled, Isla." The clan-lord's voice rumbled over her then. "What's wrong?"

She glanced his way to find that Mir-Ferrin had rolled onto his side, observing her.

"Nothing."

His mouth lifted at the corners in a half-smile. "Don't worry, we should be safe here."

"I'm not concerned about that."

"Ah, but you *are* worried about something, aren't you?"

Isla frowned. "Shut up, and mind your own business."

His smile widened, and Isla noticed that his cheek dimpled. Her pulse quickened. She'd never noticed that dimple before. She shouldn't have been surprised, for the clan-lord didn't smile often.

"After this is all over, I'll miss these conversations," he murmured.

"Really? Are you a masochist?"

"I must be," he replied, his voice lowering further, "since I'm starting to enjoy your company." He paused then, before admitting, "I can be myself around you."

Isla swallowed. "Don't say that."

He propped himself up on one elbow. "Why not? It's the truth."

Their gazes fused then, and Isla's breathing stilled.

He'd been teasing her gently just moments before. But there was no sign of humor now. Instead, his chiseled features were taut, his dark eyes intense.

"Don't look at me like that either," she whispered, cursing the way her voice caught.

He swallowed. "I can't help it."

"Yes, you can. Stop it."

Instead of replying, or complying, Mir-Ferrin leaned down and grazed his lips over hers.

Isla went rigid, her breath catching once more. She should strike him across the face for that—but she didn't.

He lowered his mouth to hers again, caressing her with the same butterfly-light pressure. His lips, soft and sensual, brushed against hers. And then he drew back, his gaze roaming over her face.

He was waiting for her response.

Isla's breathing stopped, and then need twisted deep within her. Unbidden, a shuddering sigh escaped her.

He heard it, and dipped his head once more, kissing her properly this time—firmly.

Isla couldn't help herself. Her lips parted under his, and when his tongue slid into her mouth, she moaned.

The Gods forgive her, he tasted good.

An answering groan rumbled through his chest, and before Isla knew what was happening, Mir-Ferrin's mouth was devouring hers.

All rational thought fled. Suddenly, she just wanted to escape herself, to find oblivion in this man.

Isla clawed her way into his arms, hunger spiraling through her. She pressed her body hard against his, almost as if she could crawl inside him, while she kissed him back, their tongues dueling. And when she grazed her teeth against his lower lip, a growl rumbled through his chest.

The sound set something free inside her, and she repeated the act.

Mir-Ferrin rolled over onto his back, bringing her with him—and suddenly, she was sitting astride him, rolling her hips as she ground into his groin.

He was hard for her. She could feel every inch of his impressive erection.

Rasping a curse, Mir-Ferrin reached forward, unzipping the front of her jumpsuit, and pushing it down. Panting now, Isla helped him before she yanked off the thin tank top and bra she wore underneath.

He pulled her down so that her breasts hung in his face. And when he started to suckle her, Isla let out a high, keening cry.

She'd forgotten how good this felt.

The heat of his mouth, and the way he was sucking her nipple, drawing it deep, made her squirm against him.

Delicious pleasure arrowed through her, straight between her thighs.

She had to feel him naked against her. Now. She had to lose herself in him.

Sensing her urgency, Mir-Ferrin tore his mouth from her breast and lifted her off him.

They wriggled out of their clothes, flinging them carelessly aside. Undressing wasn't easy on the squidgy make-shift mattress—and they both burst out laughing—before Isla climbed astride Mir-Ferrin once more.

And then their mirth faded.

This time there was nothing between them. This time, she could slide along the rigid length of his cock while she explored the sculpted planes of his chest with her hands.

He stared up at her, lips parted, eyes black in the pale light of the glow-lamp.

Leaning forward, letting the tips of her swollen nipples graze his chest, Isla kissed him. Their tongues tangled, and their teeth clashed, while she rolled her hips against him, grinding herself into him once more.

And now that it was just skin on skin, the delicious friction was almost unbearable.

A warm throbbing started between her thighs, building as she rubbed against him. She was wet now, so much so that she glided up and down the steel of his erection. The pleasure grew, shivering across her belly.

She needed more. She had to have him inside her.

Ripping her mouth from Mir-Ferrin's, Isla pushed herself up, breathing hard as she rose above him.

Her thighs trembled, and she fumbled with eagerness as she reached for his cock. Her fingers slid around its girth. His cock then jerked in her grip; he was as ready for this as she was.

His hands gripped her hips then, and he lifted her up so she could position him at her entrance. Once he was pressed against her, he let go of her hips, allowing her to make the next move.

Panting, Isla stared down at him.

Their gazes fused, and Isla understood. He was allowing this to be her choice, her decision. If she wanted to stop now, he'd let her go.

But Isla didn't want to stop. Right now, she felt as if she'd die if he wasn't inside her. What a relief it was not to think—to let her body take control.

With exquisite slowness, she sank down on him, impaling herself, inch by delicious inch, until their bodies were flush.

A loud groan escaped Isla then, and she arched her back, driving herself down on him as far as he'd go.

"Isla," he breathed her name like a prayer. "I'm all yours … do what you want to me. *Use* me."

His words inflamed her, caused the pulsing pleasure in her womb to throb.

She started to rock against him, gently at first so that there was just a little friction. And then, she started to ride his cock, enjoying the long, slick slide of him.

Mir-Ferrin lifted his hips with each thrust, and as he did, she arched her back, driving him deeper.

And as they moved, he reached forward and slid his thumb between her slick thighs, rubbing her gently.

Isla's choked cry filled the service shaft, echoing off the surrounding metal, while waves of warm, throbbing pleasure rippled out from where the pad of his thumb circled.

And when she tilted her pelvis back just a little farther, the head of his cock hit a sensitive spot deep inside—and Isla shattered.

Losing all sense of where she was, or whom she was with, she went wild, bucking against him as ecstasy pulsed through her and turned her body liquid.

Vaguely, she could hear a woman's raw gasps and pleas—was that her?—but she was too far gone to care. She was in a place where she could forget everything— a place she longed to remain.

Elijah stared up at the woman riding him, stunned at how beautiful, how wild, she was.

Isla had completely let go. Her supple body gleamed with sweat as she writhed and shuddered, her head falling back as another cry ripped from her.

Her breasts bobbed and swayed as she came.

Those tits had been a revelation. They were deliciously full, with large rose-colored nipples that begged to be sucked.

Shifting his hand from beneath her thighs, Elijah gripped hold of her hips with both hands. He slid her up and down his length, faster now.

A groan escaped him, and his head fell back, his eyes fluttering closed.

Gods, this felt good—better than anything he'd ever experienced.

Heat gathered in the small of his back, while pressure and excitement coiled in his groin—and then the dam burst. He'd wanted to go longer, to bring Isla to climax again before he lost control, but it was too much.

Hot pleasure pumped through him as he arched up off the mattress. A shout ripped from his throat, and he emptied himself into her.

And when the storm passed, when he collapsed, struggling to catch his breath, Elijah opened his eyes to find Isla staring down at him.

She was majestic, perched there astride him. Unforgettable. Her full lips were slightly parted, her cheeks were flushed, and her midnight-blue eyes were dark with pleasure.

Elijah's gaze met hers.

He'd felt her desperation as she'd ridden him, her need to escape—and he'd understood. And when he'd asked her to use him, he meant it.

He'd wanted her to let go, for her to forget her pain, her grief.

And when she'd lost control, so had he.

Gazing up at her, Elijah wished he could hold onto this moment, but already it was slipping away. Reality was seeping back. He wanted to keep it at bay for just a short while longer, yet he couldn't.

And maybe it was better he didn't.

The woman who'd just ridden him, who'd just given him the most powerful climax of his life, was Cathal Mir-Brennan's widow.

Elijah exhaled slowly, his eyes fluttering shut. The Gods had thrown them together, but this closeness couldn't last.

18. SHAMELESS

ISLA STIRRED, DRIFTING slowly out of a deep, delicious sleep toward wakefulness. She was comfortable and the mattress seemed to embrace her.

But as she emerged from sleep, she realized that it wasn't the crumpled survival-dome material that she was snuggling into, but a warm male body. And when her eyes flickered open, it dawned on her that she was nestling against Elijah Mir-Ferrin.

They'd left the glow-lamp on its lowest setting before going to sleep, and it illuminated the shaft in soft light.

She was in the clan-lord's arms—and they were both naked.

He lay on his back, his arms encircling her, while she curled into his side, her cheek resting upon his chest, her left leg sprawled across his thighs.

It was an intimate position—one she'd avoided the night before.

After they'd had sex, she'd rolled off him and moved away, shifting onto her side so that she faced the wall. She'd told herself she needed to put some clothes on, yet exhaustion had pulled her down into its clutches. And, clearly, while she'd been asleep, instinct had kicked in, and she'd sought the heat and strength of the man lying next to her.

Isla stiffened as her heart started to pound, the last of sleep sloughing away.

Was he awake? Maybe she could extricate herself from his embrace and wriggle away without Elijah ever knowing.

Elijah. Nain strike her down, was she thinking of him in first-name terms now?

Gently, Isla tried to ease out of his hold. However, the clan-lord's arms merely tightened around her.

"Good morning." His voice, husky with sleep, rumbled in her ear. "Did you sleep well?"

Isla went rigid against him, heat washing over her as mortification rose. "Very well, thank you," she replied through gritted teeth. "But you can let me go."

"Must I?" he murmured. "I'm very comfortable … I don't think I've ever slept so well."

"That's a relief to hear," she muttered.

He gave a soft laugh, one that made her pulse flutter in her throat.

She hadn't heard him laugh before.

She wasn't remotely drowsy now. Instead, all her senses had sharpened. She was aware of the heat and strength of his body against hers, of the musky scent of skin. The smell of him caused a melting sensation to ripple through her lower belly.

Suddenly, the desire to wrap herself around him, to slide her hands over his naked skin, and repeat what they'd done hours earlier, was overwhelming.

However, her embarrassment was stronger.

Gods damn it, she'd completely lost it the night before. How would she ever look this man in the eye ever again?

Isla shoved at his chest—and this time, he let her go.

Heart pounding, she shuffled over to where her clothing still lay scattered over their improvised mattress. Wordlessly, she wriggled into her jumpsuit and zipped up the front. She was yanking on her boots when she chanced a look in Elijah's direction.

That was a mistake.

He was putting on his pants lying down and was lifting his hips to pull them up.

Isla's breathing grew shallow at the sight—for it reminded her of how he'd arched up against her when she'd ridden him the night before.

Heat flushed over her again. Curse her, she'd been shameless.

His gaze lifted then, ensnaring hers, and she started to sweat.

"Isla." His expression was serious now. "Are you okay? Last night was—"

"Of course," she snapped, cursing how brittle her voice sounded. "Why wouldn't I be?"

Elijah pushed himself up and shuffled over to her on his knees.

Isla would have wriggled back to avoid him, but with the hopper parked behind her, there was nowhere to go.

Instead, she dropped her gaze.

A second later, his fingers trailed down her cheek, and he took hold of her chin, gently tilting her face up so that she met his eye once more. "It caught us by surprise," he murmured, "but there's no point in pretending it didn't happen."

Isla swallowed. "I'm not."

"We're both adults."

Her breathing slowed. She was acutely aware of the feel of his fingers cupping her chin. Part of her wanted to bat his hand away, while another longed to lean into his touch. "I lost control," she whispered.

"We *both* did … but I don't regret it." He paused then, his dark eyes shadowing. "Do you?"

Isla stared back at him, her throat constricting. Gods, she wanted to tell him she did, for mortification still burned a hole in her chest. However, the words wouldn't come.

The seconds drew out before she exhaled shakily. And then, to her own surprise, she shook her head.

Walking into the spaceport's terminal building, Elijah was relieved to find it busy. Heavy crowds thronged the wide domed area, and a series of announcements echoed over the rumble of voices.

Like most spaceports, the crowd was a mix of galactic races. Amongst the travelers, Elijah spied a group of black-robed figures—humans mostly, with shaven heads and solemn faces. They'd just emerged from the Arrivals terminal.

Elijah's gaze narrowed as he tracked them. They didn't need more Wis worshippers here, not after the recent riots. Estradia's position, on the fringes of his territory, made it appealing to extremists, but this city was fast becoming a pressure cooker. Word had clearly spread that the *Creed of Truth* had put down roots here.

Glancing over at Isla, Elijah noted that she'd pulled her hood down to obscure her face. He reached up and did the same with his own.

After emerging from their hiding place, leaving the hopper in the service shaft, they'd found the commercial hub open for business and thronged with shoppers. Then, before catching a trans-barge to the spaceport, they'd used some of their last credits on the PCSD to buy cloaks and some breakfast.

And now that they'd reached their destination, Elijah was relieved they'd bought the hooded cloaks. It wasn't much of a disguise, but it was the best they could do at present.

Bowing his head, and wishing he weren't so tall, Elijah cut across the wide sandstone floor to where a row of bars and eateries lined one wall. On the way, he caught sight of two battle-droids at the far end of the terminal.

They often traveled in pairs, and these two were standing at the gates, surveying the travelers joining the line to go through security.

Elijah's gaze narrowed. Fortunately for him and Isla, they wouldn't be taking a commercial flight off Estradia. They couldn't afford one anyway. Instead, during the trans-barge journey, they'd decided it was best to get off-planet on a freighter.

To do that, they needed to find a pilot who'd agree to let them earn their passage. Elijah's frown deepened. He had no doubt that would be a challenge. Most pilots preferred dealing in hard credits.

Considering this, his gaze shifted right then, alighting on a lithe man dressed in charcoal and bronze body armor.

His pulse quickened.

The individual had his back to him, yet he recognized the soldier's stalking gait, even though he limped slightly this morning.

Elijah slowed his stride and moved close to Isla. "A friend of ours is here," he murmured. "Near the departure board."

Isla glanced in the direction he'd indicated before she swore under her breath. "Shit. I'd hoped you'd killed him."

"So did I."

They halted a moment, in the midst of the busy terminal.

"Security's tight in here this morning," Isla muttered, her gaze continuing to sweep their surroundings.

"It is," Elijah agreed. "Especially with all the Wis devotees flooding in … look."

Indeed, another wave of black-robed figures had just swept out from Arrivals.

He became aware then of the tension that rippled across the cavernous domed space. At first, he'd thought it was due to the battle-droids, but then he spied figures clad in dark-bronze body armor, laser rifles at their sides, circling the space. The Crelcaster Guard had a particularly heavy presence this morning. Something told Elijah that—unlike the battle-droids and that marine—most of those guards weren't hunting him.

Instead, they were watching the followers of Wis.

"Right," Isla murmured. "I suppose this is a good thing for us though. It makes us harder to spot."

"It does," he agreed. "Come on, there's a bar over there. Two Rendak, who look like freighter pilots, have just gone in. We might find someone who needs crew."

Isla followed Elijah through the crowd toward the bar.

Frowning, she surveyed the shabby façade. On the way here, the plan they'd come up with—to strike a deal with a cargo ship pilot—was the best they could manage.

However, now that they were inside the spaceport, Isla worried it wouldn't work. You couldn't trust the scum you met in these places. She also doubted many freighter pilots would be interested; they preferred paying passengers to those who wanted to work for it.

Her attention shifted to where Elijah was stepping through the entranceway. Noting the tense set of his shoulders, her frown deepened.

This wasn't going to be easy.

Inside the bar, she breathed in the cloying scent of clove smoke and surveyed the dimly lit interior. A few roughly dressed individuals sprawled at booths around the edge of the space. Some smoked clove pipes, while others ate breakfast. Serving-droids floated from table to table, taking orders and dishing up platters of food.

Elijah was also scanning the room, and his gaze settled upon the two Rendak he'd mentioned earlier. They stared back at him. Thin tongues darted from lipless mouths, their eyes glinting.

Isla moved closer to Elijah. And then, without thinking, she reached out, wrapping her fingers around his wrist. "Rendak can be unscrupulous," she warned. "If they discover you're a hunted man, they'll think they can make some credits out of you."

"Point taken." Elijah shifted his gaze to the other booths. "I'd rather" —he broke off then, his arm going rigid under her grip— "Jidea be praised," he whispered. "I think I've found our way off Estradia."

Releasing Elijah's wrist, Isla peered through the fug of clove smoke. He was staring at a human female seated at a booth at the far end of the bar.

Small, with short curly light-auburn hair, and dressed in dark-grey cargos and utility vest, she blended in easily with the shadows.

The woman hadn't seen them. Instead, her attention was focused on the tablet she was scrolling through. A tray of empty dishes sat in front of her.

Isla cut Elijah another look, to see that he wore a thin smile. "Do you know her?"

"Oh, yes."

Without another word, he set off across the floor.

19. FRIEND OR FOE

"GOOD MORNING, GRETA," Elijah greeted the pilot, sliding into the booth opposite her.

Outwardly, he was calm, yet his heart now kicked against his ribs.

He couldn't believe his luck.

Two years had passed since he'd last seen this woman—yet he hadn't forgotten her face.

Isla took a seat next to him in the booth. Her gaze flicked between them. No doubt, she was curious to know what he was up to. But she'd find out soon enough.

He'd been worried about how exactly he was going to convince a pilot to assist them—yet the moment he'd spotted the woman in the corner, his concern lifted.

Greta flattened herself against the back of the booth, the tablet she'd been staring at thumping onto the table. "Raul's balls," she whispered. "Elijah Mir-Ferrin."

"That's right," he replied. "Didn't expect to ever see me again, did you?"

Greta's round face, with its scattering of freckles across the bridge of her nose, turned the color of ash. Her throat then bobbed. "I thought you were dead … wasn't your battleship destroyed a few days ago?"

Heat flushed through Elijah. Of course, Greta knew about that—as he'd seen at *Rosa's Inn,* the destruction of *Defiance* had been broadcast on news-reels throughout the sector.

"It was … but unluckily for you, I survived."

"Are you going to introduce us?" Isla spoke up then, her voice cool.

Elijah's gaze didn't waver from the woman opposite.

"Isla, meet Greta Mir-Hamil. She's the pilot who helped Aria Mir-Straken and Vic Mir-Riorde escape Platinum 5."

Isla gave a soft gasp. "Really?"

"Really."

Greta's gaze flicked from Elijah to Isla, her hands sliding across the tabletop.

"Keep your hands where I can see them, Greta," Elijah snapped. "I've got a laser-pistol pointed your way under the table."

Indeed, he'd slid his gun out of its holster, although he'd shifted the energy output down to 'stun'. Greta wasn't any good to him dead.

He had plans for her.

The pilot froze, beads of sweat now appearing on her upper lip. "I didn't know what they'd done," she gasped out after a pause. "The cyborg bought passage off the space station … that's it. I didn't want to get involved in anything illegal."

"That didn't stop you from helping him tie me up and shut me in that locker."

A nerve flickered in Greta's cheek. "I didn't want to do it … he *insisted*."

A heartbeat passed before Elijah asked, "Do you remember what I said I'd do to you, if I ever caught up with you?"

Even two years on, he'd never forget the humiliation of that incident. He'd been halfway through threatening to put Greta and her Gibbit copilot before a firing squad when the cyborg had punched him in the stomach. Then, before he could recover his breath, Aria had sealed his mouth with tape.

Greta nodded.

"Well, the Gods are smiling upon you, for I'm in a merciful mood. You're not going to die today … instead, you're going to help me and my friend out."

Greta's grey eyes widened. "What?"

"We need to get off-planet … and you're going to take us wherever we wish to go."

The sounds of shouting, followed by the ping of laser fire, intruded then, filtering through the open door of the bar.

"What the—" Isla began before screaming cut her off.

"Time to go," Elijah grunted.

Isla leaped to her feet, as did Greta. However, an instant later, Elijah was at the pilot's side, the butt of his pistol jamming into the small of her back. "Come on … let's get to the gate."

Greta's mouth thinned, her grey eyes narrowing. Yet a nudge from Elijah made her obey.

The three of them left the bar, pushing their way through the crowd that was gathering at its entrance.

All gazes were trained upon the center of the terminal floor, where a group of black-robed figures was battling the Crelcaster Guard.

And as Elijah looked on, one of the robed men ignited a laser-blade and plunged it through the throat of the guard who'd tried to subdue him.

"Unbeliever!" the devotee howled, his voice cutting through the din. "You cannot stand in the way of the Truth!"

The guard crumpled, while around them more screams echoed high into the domed roof of the spaceport.

Elijah frowned. He didn't know how the fight had started or who was to blame—but it had quickly turned deadly.

More armored figures burst into the terminal then. The Crelcaster Guard now outnumbered the Followers of Wis considerably. They swarmed around the pilgrims.

Elijah's heart jolted against his breastbone. It was clear which way this struggle was going to go, but in the meantime, the chaos had created a diversion.

One he wouldn't waste.

He pushed Greta toward the gate that led out to the private berths and cargo bays.

"Keep moving," he growled when Greta tried to slow her step.

"Get your IDs ready then," she replied, biting out the words. They were approaching the gate now, where a droid had parked itself, waiting to check their identification cards.

"I don't have one on me," he answered. It was true. Unlike his crew onboard *Defiance*, Elijah didn't have any need to carry an ID on him. A retinal scan gave him access to any high-security areas.

He glanced over at Isla, and she shook her head. "I lost mine while we were fighting onboard your ship."

Greta shot them both a disbelieving look. "Well, you won't be going anywhere without IDs." Relief sparked in the pilot's eyes; she obviously thought their lack of IDs would prevent Elijah and Isla from leaving with her.

However, she was wrong.

"We'll jump the turnstiles then," Elijah shot back.

"What?"

"You heard me ... you go first." He shoved her forward. "We'll be right behind you."

Greta cursed.

"Go!"

The pilot lurched forward covering the last few yards to the gate and the row of turnstiles in front of it. The droid let out a shrill bleep, its metal arms flailing. However, Greta dodged its grasp and vaulted over the turnstiles.

Elijah and Isla followed her.

Alarms went off—but as Elijah had hoped, the pitched battle behind them drowned the blaring claxons out.

However, as he'd also suspected, the moment she'd jumped the barrier, Greta tried to take off.

She'd gotten a few yards distant when Elijah tackled her to the floor.

Picking himself up, he hauled Greta to her feet and slammed the butt of the laser-pistol into her spine once more. "No, you don't. Keep moving!"

The three of them ran through the network of covered passageways beyond the terminal, and past a series of walkways leading out to landing bays. Meanwhile, sirens rang out over the whole spaceport now.

Greta led them to a small bay where a sleek D-Class freighter sat on a landing pad. With its narrow nose, the ship had the classic shape of all Mir-Ferrin ships.

Elijah scowled.

He recalled Greta's cargo ship two years ago as a Mir-Lelith rust-bucket: *CS Vertigo*. But the name on the Lazda-steel hull of this freighter was *CS Intrepid*.

In the months after the *CS Vertigo* had departed Platinum 5, Elijah had hunted for the ship. No wonder he hadn't been able to track it down though—Greta had changed freighter.

Clattering up the lowered ramp, they turned left into a passageway. In the cabin beyond, a wiry, hirsute figure sprawled on one of the bunks, snoring loudly.

Despite that their entrance hadn't been quiet, Greta's first mate was oblivious.

"Frol!" Greta snapped. "Get up!"

The Gibbit jolted awake, a high-pitched squeal tearing from its throat when its gaze settled on Elijah. "Mir-Ferrin!"

Elijah glanced Frol's way as he maneuvered Greta up to the cockpit. "Get your ass into that copilot's chair."

Moments later, Greta and Frol were sitting side-by-side, rapidly going through their preflight checks, while Elijah stood behind them, watching every move.

Isla stepped up next to him then, nudging him with her elbow to gain his attention. "Where are we headed?" Her voice was tight, wary.

Elijah knew why. She expected him to take them to Platinum 5—and probably worried he'd betray her.

Isla didn't need to be concerned about being double-crossed. He'd given her his word—and he wouldn't go back on it. However, he *had* been tempted to tell Greta to set coordinates for the space station. Yet he hesitated.

Lucas was smart—even though he wasn't likely to have been sworn in as clan-lord yet, he'd have ensured that all the battle-droids guarding Alpha Deck were reprogrammed to take orders from *him* by now.

They might be under orders to kill Elijah on sight.

Elijah didn't know who friend or foe was any longer. He had to be one step ahead of his treacherous brother. Instinct told him, it wouldn't be wise to return to Platinum 5 right now.

And so, he held Isla's gaze. "Where's Lady Jenna residing at the moment?" he asked.

"Staturine II … her new residence on Idral won't be ready for a few months yet." Isla paused then, her brow furrowing. "Why?"

Elijah shifted his attention to where Greta had just ignited the engines. The deck beneath his feet started to vibrate and the engine pitch rose as they readied themselves for take-off.

"Get us out of here fast," he instructed. "And then, as soon as we clear Estradia's orbit, set a course for Staturine II in the Frastar System."

20. LETTING GO

"STATURINE II?" ISLA wasn't sure she'd heard him correctly.

Elijah's gaze didn't waver. "That's right."

"Why?"

His mouth quirked. "Don't you want to see your daughter?"

Isla's heart started to pound. Of course, she did. However, she couldn't believe that given his shot at going anywhere in the sector, Elijah would choose the heart of Mir-Brennan territory.

Meanwhile, the engines had reached a high whine.

"Strap yourselves in," Greta ordered, her voice clipped. "This won't be smooth."

Elijah nodded before holstering his laser-pistol. "I'll be watching you, Greta," he warned. "Don't try anything foolish."

Letting his words lie, Elijah moved back to the row of seats in the cabin.

Wordlessly, Isla joined him, and they both clipped themselves in.

Moments later, the freighter started to lift off the landing pad. Meanwhile, the comm on the instrument panel had started to beep frantically.

Tower Control had noticed that the *CS Intrepid* was making an unscheduled departure.

"Don't answer that," Elijah called out.

The freighter rose off the landing pad before swiveling around and accelerating upward. Isla peered forward, catching a glimpse of the enormous receding dome of Crelcaster spaceport surrounded by mustard-colored dirt.

Her stomach dropped then as the freighter shot upward, through the planet's atmosphere.

The comm, which had momentarily fallen silent, started beeping again, hysterically this time.

Up ahead, the outline of a sleek Mir-Ferrin battleship hove into sight, in orbit around the planet.

"That'll be *Dominion* calling," Elijah spoke up once more. "My brother's ship. Don't answer them either."

"They'll lock us in a tractor beam if I don't reply," Greta snapped. Her fingers now flew over the console as she calculated their route.

"Not if you make the jump into hyperspace first."

The pilot growled a string of curses, yet her hands didn't still.

"Hurry up." Elijah didn't take his gaze from the pilot. "We're getting too close."

"Almost done," Greta replied between gritted teeth. She then glanced at her copilot. "Ready, Frol?"

"Ready," the Gibbit rasped.

Greta's shoulders tensed as she hauled down on a lever, and the freighter lurched forward, throwing them all back in their seats. In an instant, the Mir-Ferrin battleship disappeared, as did one of Estradia's golden moons hovering on the far-right edge of the cockpit window. Stars now flowed past in distorted silver streams.

Heaving a shuddering sigh of relief, Isla sank back in her seat.

Gods, they'd made it.

She couldn't believe it.

Since Elijah had approached Greta in that bar, events had moved so swiftly she was having trouble keeping up.

And now they were headed to Staturine II.

She turned her head right then, her gaze settling upon the man next to her. "So," she murmured. "Are you going to tell me why you're delivering yourself to the Mir-Brennans?"

He favored her with a half-smile. "I decided it was time."

Isla inclined her head, incredulity feathering through her. "Time for what, exactly?"

Their gazes held, and warmth ignited in Isla's belly. There was an intimacy in that look, reminding her of what they'd shared the night before.

"A fresh start," he murmured.

Isla swallowed, the heat creeping up to her chest. To cover up her discomfort, she raised an eyebrow. "You mean, you'd consider peace between the Mir-Brennans and the Mir-Ferrins?"

He nodded. "I never thought I would … but spending time with you has changed my perspective, Isla. If you and I can work together, maybe Lady Jenna and I can too."

Isla stared back at him. Was he serious?

"And you think Jenna will want to talk to you … after everything that's happened?"

Silence fell between them, their conversation replaced by the hum of the engines. Greta and Frol were ignoring their passengers as they were busy checking readouts and displays on the console.

"Probably not," Elijah replied, his gaze not wavering from hers, "but it's worth a shot."

Hands cupped around a tumbler of Morith whisky, Isla focused on the woman seated opposite her at the table. She then flashed Greta a half-smile. "We didn't get off on the right foot earlier," she murmured. "I just wanted to apologize … Elijah was a bit heavy-handed back there."

Across the cabin, the clan-lord muttered something under his breath. Elijah was leaning up against the bulkhead, watching Frol complete checks in the cockpit. "I did what was necessary."

Greta's mouth pursed. She then raised her own glass to her lips and took a large gulp before answering, "I don't think we've been introduced."

"I'm Isla … Cathal Mir-Brennan's widow."

Greta tensed, her grey eyes—the smoky hue of Lazda-steel—snapping wide. "Gods, what are *you* doing hanging around with the Mir-Ferrin clan-lord?"

Isla's mouth quirked once more. "It's a long story." She leaned forward then. "Aria and Vic got to safety because of you … thank you."

Spots of high color rose onto Greta's cheeks. "Vic paid me well," she muttered. She then raised a hand, gesturing around her. "He was so desperate that he gave me his ship … *The Wayfarer.* I re-registered it under a new name though."

"Ah," Elijah spoke up once more. "I was wondering what happened to that wreck you owned two years ago."

Isla glanced Elijah's way, meeting his eye. "You should know that Vic Mir-Riorde now leads Lady Jenna's personal bodyguard … both he and Aria live at Castle Valnor on Staturine II. If you want to meet with Jenna, I hope you're ready to face them too."

He tensed, and Isla understood right then that he wasn't. "It looks like I'm not the only one with revenge issues," she murmured.

"I have no idea what you're talking about," Greta interrupted them. The pilot's gaze flicked between Elijah and Isla, a deep groove between her finely arched eyebrows. "And I don't really care … but" —she swallowed hard— "I need to know what you're going to do with me when we reach our destination."

Elijah's dark brows crashed together. "You—"

"You'll be free to go," Isla smoothly cut him off, while finishing his sentence.

"Really?" Greta didn't look convinced, and in her place, Isla wouldn't have been either. Especially since Elijah was now glowering at them.

"*Really,*" Isla replied, her voice firm. She then looked back at Elijah, and their gazes met once more. It was an irony that she understood what drove this man—but right now, it was like looking into a mirror. "If you want change, then you need to let *everything* go." She paused, her throat tightening. "I've had to."

21. A WELCOMING COMMITTEE

"PERMISSION TO LAND at Castle Valnor denied, *CS Intrepid*." The officious voice crackled over the comm. "Please contact Tower Control at Briscay spaceport. You are to request permission to land there."

Greta pressed the mute button on the comm, huffed a sigh, and cast the man and woman standing behind her an exasperated look. "I told you they wouldn't let me land at the castle."

"Let me speak to them," Isla replied, her tone clipped.

She hadn't wanted to let *Star Tempest* know she was aboard this freighter. She'd have preferred to slip back into the castle without fanfare. However, Greta was right. They were never going to let a Mir-Ferrin cargo ship land at the clan-lady's private residence.

It had been a long journey in hyperspace to Staturine II—nearly twenty hours. During that time, Isla had gotten gradually tenser, anticipating her arrival.

"Go on then." Greta punched the comm once more.

Leaning in, Isla cleared her throat. "*Star Tempest,* this is Isla Mir-Brennan … I urgently request clearance to land at Castle Valnor."

The comm crackled a moment, and when the comms officer replied, his voice had lost its bureaucratic edge. "My Lady?" Concern crept in. "Are you well?"

"Yes, thank you," she replied crisply. "Rest assured, I'm not in any trouble … and please inform the clan-lady that I'll be on-planet shortly."

"Yes, My Lady." Another pause followed. "Permission to land at Castle Valnor granted, *CS Intrepid*. You can make your approach when ready."

With a nod to Greta, Isla drew back and returned to the row of seats in the cabin.

Elijah joined her.

Together, they buckled themselves in, while in the cockpit, Greta and Frol prepared to enter Staturine II's atmosphere.

The planet itself filled the void beneath them, its surface swirls of cream, fawn, and blue. And to the far left of the cockpit window, the bulky outline of the clan-lady's flagship, *Star Tempest*, orbited the planet.

"I expected you to look happier about coming back here," Elijah commented then, his voice low.

Isla glanced up from where she'd just finished adjusting her harness. She then frowned. "I *am* happy."

He cocked an eyebrow. "You're nervous about facing your sister-in-law again, aren't you?"

Isla snorted, even as her stomach clenched. "A little." She pulled a face then. "Jenna will have been searching for me. She'll be relieved to know I'm alive, but she'll also be angry."

"Don't tell me you're scared of her?"

Isla stiffened. "I'm not." And she wasn't. However, the Mir-Brennan clan-lady wasn't a woman lightly crossed. Jenna's soft, feminine appearance hid a will of iron. "But she'd be right to be pissed off. I took off without a word, abandoned my daughter." Isla raised a hand and rubbed at her eyes. Gods, she *was* nervous.

There wasn't any decent excuse she could give— especially since she was bringing the man that she'd set out to kill back with her. Of course, she could double-cross Elijah and tell Jenna she'd brought her the ultimate hostage. Yet something in her refused to take that path.

Whatever his motive, Elijah was doing the right thing, and she wanted to help him.

But although she was nervous about how Jenna would react to seeing the clan-lord, she was more worried about how Bea would respond.

Would her daughter even want to see her? Bea was sensitive—and she'd likely started to believe her mother was dead.

Everyone would think she'd lost her mind.

And Isla wondered the same thing. She'd set out to assassinate Elijah Mir-Ferrin, yet not only had they become unlikely allies of sorts, but she'd also had sex with him.

Their gazes held now, and Elijah's closeness was doing strange things to Isla's pulse. She could feel the heat of his thigh just a couple of inches from hers.

"It's strange," she said then, her voice barely above a whisper. "I'm not used to feeling anything except anger. The need to 'get even' consumed me completely for so long, it's like I've forgotten who I am."

"You know who you are, Isla." His hand lifted then, from where it rested on his thigh, as if he intended to touch her. However, likely realizing that would be a mistake, he lowered it again. "You're a warrior."

Isla's breathing grew shallow. She was at a loss for how to answer him. And the Gods damn them both, there was a part of her that wished he *had* placed his hand over hers.

Elijah's mouth curved, although his gaze remained serious. "Just be honest with your family when you see them ... they'll understand."

The freighter shuddered then, warning them they were entering Staturine II's atmosphere.

Isla swallowed, the pressure in her chest increasing. She wished he wouldn't be so understanding.

Having sex with Elijah was a mistake—but as she'd admitted to him in that service shaft, she didn't regret it. After such a dark time, there had been something incredibly life-affirming about their encounter. For the first time in a long while, she'd let herself go, she'd let sensation rule.

But it was over now.

Just like hatred and bitterness, she had to leave it behind her.

"So, you're just letting me go?"

Greta stood in front of the cockpit, arms folded across her chest, eyeing her uninvited passengers. Her features were taut, her eyes narrowed. Behind her, Frol was also watching Isla and Elijah distrustfully. The Gibbit's spidery hands were clenched at its sides, its small frame quivering with anxiety.

Despite that Elijah hadn't threatened either of them since they'd made the jump into hyperspace, the Gibbit didn't trust him.

Its keen gaze kept flicking to the holstered laser-pistol on Elijah's thigh.

Isla didn't reply. Instead, she glanced over at Elijah, letting him reassure the pair.

After all, he was the one who'd hijacked this freighter at gunpoint. Isla didn't blame Greta for thinking she was still his prisoner.

They'd landed in the clan-lady's private landing bay at Castle Valnor. Beyond the cockpit window, Isla could see black-clad figures approaching—the Lady's Watch was coming out to meet her.

Isla's pulse quickened, sweat beading on her top lip.

Meanwhile, Greta and the Mir-Ferrin clan-lord were still eyeballing each other.

"Yes," Elijah said after a lengthy pause. He glanced Isla's way then, his mouth quirking, before focusing on the pilot once more. "You can go."

Greta's brow furrowed. "You're not going to put out a warrant on me?"

"No."

"You can stay here for a few days, if you want ... as my guests," Isla offered then, smiling.

Greta's frown deepened. She clearly didn't like that idea.

"I think we'll just get going now," the pilot replied, her tone clipped. "I was waiting for a shipment on Estradia. I ... need to get back there."

"Right." Elijah shifted his attention back to Isla. "You've got a welcoming committee waiting outside. Shall we go out to meet them?"

Jenna Mir-Brennan's lips parted, her brown eyes—the color of polished mahogany—snapping wide. An instant later, her heart-shaped face paled.

Isla's pulse quickened at Jenna's reaction. Of course, she would think a ghost stood before her. Elijah Mir-Ferrin was supposed to have gone down with his flagship.

The silence in the landing bay drew out. A small crowd had gathered around the freighter. Just behind Jenna stood a tall dark-haired man with bright violet eyes—the clan-lady's consort, Malik. Like his wife, Malik's expression was stunned as he stared at the new arrivals.

Black-armored figures surrounded them, and one of them, a well-built man with an eye plant embedded in his right eye socket, and a blood-red sand scarab embossed upon his breastplate, stepped forward.

As always, Vic's face was expressionless as his single hazel eye swept over Isla and speared the man standing next to her. The rest of his guards watched Elijah, their visored gazes gleaming in the harsh lights inside the hangar. Their bodies were rigid, their hands resting on the grips of their laser-blades—ready for action.

When the Captain of the Lady's Watch finally spoke, his voice was incredulous. "What. The. Fuck?"

Isla swallowed to try and ease the sudden tightness in her throat. "I should explain."

She was grateful that Elijah didn't speak.

"Yes, Isla," Jenna said finally, her tone brittle. "I'd think you'd better."

"Is a bit complicated," Isla replied, attempting to smile at her sister-in-law, and failing.

"We're all listening."

Isla drew in a deep, steadying breath. She supposed it was best to start at the beginning. And so, she did. She started talking, and as she explained how revenge had consumed her—how she'd trained rigorously for the express purpose of hunting Elijah and Lucas Mir-Ferrin—a deep groove formed between Jenna's eyebrows. Her jaw had tensed, as if she was forcing herself not to interrupt. However, the clan-lady had demanded an explanation and would let Isla finish.

Jenna was an expert diplomat and had worked as her brother's ambassador before his death. Even so, remaining silent was costing her.

Isla continued her tale, describing how she'd boarded *Defiance* as a technician and lived aboard for a while before making her move. She then told them about her assassination attempt and the explosions that had foiled it—explaining how their escape pod had crash-landed on Estradia.

Isla stopped there. All gazes were on her, and a deep silence had fallen in the landing bay. Glancing over her shoulder, she saw Greta and Frol standing at the top of the ramp inside the freighter.

Her tale had drawn them out too.

Heaving in a deep breath, Isla continued, detailing how Mir-Ferrin had taken her prisoner, how they'd fought off the soldiers his brother had sent after him. She finished her story by explaining how they'd managed to get off Estradia.

And when she finally concluded, she was sweating. The faces surrounding her didn't look any friendlier. Of course, there was far more to this story—so many details that she'd left out. But she was done for the moment.

"Mir-Ferrin could have gone anywhere, but he wanted to come here," she said, meeting Jenna's eye. "He's not my hostage ... he's here of his free will ... and he wants to speak to you."

22. TRUST IS EARNED

ELIJAH WALKED TO the window and looked out. The view from the clan-lady's solar, high up in Castle Valnor, was a spectacular one. He gazed across a dove-grey skyline of spires and domes with snow-capped mountains behind. The sun was setting, painting the pale sky with ribbons of mauve and rose-pink.

However, it was difficult to concentrate on the view, what with stares stabbing into his back.

Isla had done an admirable job of diffusing the tension in the landing bay upon their arrival.

It had been hard for Elijah to keep silent, not to step in and attempt to take control of the situation. Nonetheless, he'd read the room earlier. Vic Mir-Riorde's hand had rested on the hilt of his laser-blade, his fingers flexing. The cyborg had been close to drawing the weapon—and using it. Elijah's own fingers had twitched, and he'd resisted the urge to let his hand stray to the grip of his laser-pistol.

But now he was upstairs, standing in Jenna Mir-Brennan's inner sanctum.

"Speak then." Malik's voice rumbled across the large chamber. "We're all listening."

Elijah turned from the window, his gaze sweeping over those inside the solar.

Isla sat on a sofa a few feet away. Although she appeared to be reclining, her lean form was tense. They'd come straight here from the landing bay—Isla hadn't even had time to see her daughter first.

Everyone else in the solar was standing.

The cyborg remained near the doors, legs slightly apart, hand on the hilt of his laser-blade. Elijah had been relieved of his weapon before being allowed inside the castle—but that didn't mean the Captain of the Lady's Watch had lowered *his* guard.

Lady Jenna and her husband stood a few yards back. Malik's gaze was narrowed. Like Vic, he carried a laser-blade at his side. Of course, the former bodyguard knew how to use the weapon.

Elijah didn't focus on Malik though, but on the clan-lady. Jenna's expression wasn't friendly, and neither was her gaze. This wouldn't be easy.

"Surely, you realize I'm the lesser of two evils," he said finally. "You might not like me … but you don't want Lucas in charge."

"Too late." Jenna's voice was clipped. "He's sitting in your chair … and is due to be sworn in any day now."

Elijah's pulse quickened at this reminder. "And do you want to leave things that way?"

Silence followed these words.

"I made a mistake not shutting down his research the moment I stepped into my father's role," he admitted after a pause. "I realize that now … but what matters is that I *did* put an end to it."

Jenna's eyes narrowed. "And I'm supposed to applaud you for that?"

She was trying to provoke him. The clan-lady didn't believe he was sincere; she'd been married to his younger brother, after all. When Jenna had announced her intention to divorce Tian, he'd hired assassins to kill her.

Tension rippled through Elijah. She thought he was playing her—and in her place, he'd have suspected the same. "No," he replied softly.

His stomach hardened then. What was he even doing here?

The rift between the Mir-Ferrins and the Mir-Brennans was too deep to be easily repaired. Too much blood had been spilled of late, and ever since he'd stepped into the role of clan-lord, ever since he'd dealt with this woman as an adversary, Elijah had learned that you underestimated her at your peril. Cathal had been a strong leader, yet he could be impetuous at times, hot-headed. But not Jenna. She thought everything through.

She didn't let her temper get the better of her, and her successful strike on Idral recently had proven she was an able military strategist.

But Elijah wasn't giving up either. "I don't expect you to trust me," he continued. "Not yet, anyway. Trust is earned."

Jenna's jaw flexed. "It certainly is."

"What would it take then," he said, holding her eye, "for peace to be forged between our clans?" Her mouth thinned; once again, she suspected he was trying to manipulate her. Elijah sighed. "I mean it. What do you need from me?"

Another silence fell in the solar.

Elijah was aware that all gazes were on him. He didn't glance Isla's way, yet he felt her presence. It reassured him.

Everyone else in this room hated him, but she didn't—not any longer.

The irony wasn't lost on him.

"A treaty," Jenna replied after a long pause. "Signed by every Mir-Ferrin governor … and yourself … promising not to conspire or take up arms against the Mir-Brennans, ever again. You will open the shipping lanes through the Falwae Quadrant … and you will remove all the spies you have in Mir-Brennan territory."

Malik inhaled sharply, and when Elijah glanced his way, he marked the warning look the clan-lady's consort flashed her.

Elijah inclined his head. "And what about the eyes you have on Platinum 5?" Her expression didn't alter. Nevertheless, her gaze widened just a fraction. "I'm not an idiot, Lady Jenna … Aria couldn't have gotten into that virology lab without assistance from the inside." He paused then. "If you agree to withdraw your spies, I shall do the same. Make sure all your requirements are written down in a document for me to address."

Jenna frowned. "Your father signed and then broke agreements, Mir-Ferrin. How do I know you won't do the same?"

"You don't," he replied, his half-smile fading. "And I have no way of proving to you at present that I'm a man of my word … all I can do is ask you to trust me."

Jenna snorted. "You ask too much."

"You *can* trust him."

Elijah's attention swiveled right, to where Isla sat. His breathing caught; he hadn't expected her to speak up in his defense.

Isla wasn't looking his way. Her expression was veiled, yet her blue eyes were bright as she met Jenna's gaze. "I know he's a Mir-Ferrin, but he's not like the rest of them," Isla continued, her voice oddly flat. "He's not like Tian."

Jenna sucked in a sharp breath. Meanwhile, Malik scowled.

Only Vic's expression didn't change.

Exhaling slowly, Elijah shifted his focus back to the clan-lady. She was staring at Isla, her gaze clouded with confusion. Moments passed, and then Jenna looked over at Elijah once more. "You've clearly done a number on my sister-in-law," she murmured, "but I'm not so easily convinced." Her eyebrows drew together then. "You're self-serving, just like your predecessors … and you're only here because you want our help. Because you're *desperate.*"

Elijah held her gaze. "I am." There wasn't any point in denying it. His pulse accelerated, heat igniting in the pit of his stomach. "As you would be in my place, Lady Jenna. My brother tried to assassinate me before seizing power." His mouth twisted. "I didn't *have* to come here," he reminded her, their stare drawing out. "But maybe I'm sincere … maybe I really do want change."

"Bea!"

Isla halted, her gaze alighting upon a small figure clad in a deep-pink jumpsuit, standing at the end of the hallway.

She opened her arms to hug her, but Bea didn't move.

Instead, her daughter stared at her, wide-eyed. "Ma?"

"Yes, it's me, darling."

Bea didn't move.

Vision blurring, Isla dropped her arms and took a tentative step forward. "I've missed you so much." It was clear now that her daughter wasn't going to barrel down the corridor and fling herself into her mother's embrace.

"Where have you been?" There was no missing the accusation in Bea's voice, the hurt.

Isla's throat constricted. She'd feared her daughter might react this way.

She'd really messed up.

A tall, statuesque woman with copper skin and chestnut hair stepped out of the bedchamber behind Bea then. Aria smiled at Isla, although her emerald eyes were shadowed.

Isla swallowed hard. "I suppose I've got some explaining to do."

Bea's face grew taut, her dark-blue eyes glittering. "You just disappeared, Ma. You didn't even say goodbye."

Silence followed these words. Isla couldn't deny them either—for they were the truth. "I did," she whispered, "And I'm sorry … that was wrong."

"We thought the worst, Isla," Aria said gently. A groove had appeared between her brows as she placed a reassuring hand on Bea's shoulder.

Isla's heart started to kick against her ribs. Of course, they had. She'd disappeared without a trace—and hadn't sent word to reassure them she was alive over the past months.

The selfishness of her behavior slapped her hard around the face.

Now that she'd emerged from the obsession that had driven her to hunt down the Mir-Ferrin clan-lord, she knew the truth of it: she'd risked never returning to Bea.

She'd come close to dying a few times in the past days—she'd deliberately put herself in mortal danger. At the time, her rage had blinded her, but the reality was that her chance of survival had been low. She'd had an escape route planned out, but there had always been a high risk.

She'd just convinced herself otherwise.

Isla sucked in a shaky breath, meeting her daughter's eye once more. "I was in a dark place, love," she said huskily. On the way back to Staturine II, onboard the *CS Intrepid*, she'd gone through what she'd say to her daughter. The truth was too raw—but now, she couldn't let herself lie. Not to Bea. She was old enough to hear it. "After your dad died, I was very sad. I was also angry. I couldn't accept that he was gone … and I wanted to make those responsible pay."

"But they were killed," Bea murmured. "In that blast."

Isla nodded. Of course, she was referring to Mican and Tian Mir-Ferrin. "They were," she said, her voice roughening further. "But that wasn't enough for me. I wanted the rest of their family to die … I told myself I was doing it for your dad. I told myself his death needed to be avenged."

Bea's gaze snapped wider still. The girl stepped back then, moving closer to Aria, and taking her hand as if seeking reassurance. "And did you kill them, Ma?"

Isla shook her head, her vision blurring once more. She deserved her daughter's anger, yet it cut her deep to see how little she trusted her now. "No … although I tried." She sucked in a sharp breath. "But I've let it go now. Revenge won't bring your dad back. My place is here with you … and I promise I'll never disappear like that again."

23. ON EDGE

ELIJAH SAT DOWN at the long, gleaming table and wondered if he was a guest or a prisoner this evening.

Judging from the two black armored figures that took up their posts, on either side of him, he decided it was the latter.

Around him, the others were taking their seats. None of them sat anywhere near him. There were at least three meters between him and the nearest seat.

Jenna and Malik had just taken their places at the other end of the table, directly opposite him—flanked by Aria and Vic on one side and Isla and her daughter on the other. Meanwhile, serving-droids circuited the table, filling flutes with sparkling wine and laying out appetizers.

Like the table that dominated it, the dining room was long and narrow, with a tall floor-to-ceiling window at one end. Murals decorated the walls: Fara, Goddess of Light, on one and her dark sister, Nain, upon the opposite wall.

Elijah leaned back in his chair and tried to relax. However, it was hard to.

Ever since he'd stepped off Greta's ship and entered Castle Valnor, he'd had an escort. It didn't surprise him. However, it was still disconcerting to be shadowed everywhere. The only place the two members of the Lady's Watch didn't follow him was into the quarters he'd been given.

Turning slightly, he glanced then over his shoulder at the vista beyond the large window. They were high up in Castle Valnor here. The fortress was impressive, with artistic flourishes at every corner. The hallway ceilings were all spider-vaulted—a Mir-Brennan touch—and exquisite paintings and statues lined the walls.

Outdoors, it was starting to get dark, a monochrome sky fading into indigo, and a sea of glittering lights illuminated Briscay's skyline.

This city, and castle, had an austere beauty to them.

Elijah was the first of the Mir-Ferrin ruling family to set foot here in four generations.

Considering this, he turned back to the table, to see that everyone was watching him. Their faces were all stern; it looked like he wasn't the only one on edge this evening.

His gaze met Aria's then, the tension in his stomach drawing tighter. Of course, he'd suspected their paths would cross sooner or later. He hadn't enjoyed being united with Vic Mir-Riorde again. Despite that Elijah was trying to let the need to revenge himself on the cyborg go, he'd still clenched his jaw at the sight of him.

Yet Elijah's relationship with Aria was different.

The two of them shared a history.

Their stare drew out, and Aria lifted her chin, pushing a lock of chestnut hair off her face. Next to her, Vic's jaw hardened. His expression was still blank, yet there was no mistaking the animosity, the warning, that rippled off him.

He was clearly territorial where Aria was concerned, and Elijah couldn't blame him for that. After all, Aria had once been engaged to Elijah.

However, Vic's worries were unfounded.

Elijah had long since accepted the truth—that the pair of them had never been suited. They'd known each other since childhood. Aria Mir-Straken had been his friend, his confidant. Even when they were teenagers, there hadn't been any attraction between them. Nonetheless, when their fathers arranged their marriage, Elijah had been pleased.

As they'd both matured, he'd noticed how his friend had blossomed, and had started to imagine Aria in a different light. He'd looked forward to taking their relationship into new territory.

Yet that desire was gone now.

And seeing the pair of them together didn't dredge up the old anger, the sense of betrayal that had gnawed at him after Aria and Vic had taken him captive, tied him up, and left him in a storage locker in one of the landing bays on Platinum 5 while they escaped.

He hadn't forgotten, yet he couldn't find it within him to care.

Not any longer.

Elijah's attention shifted then to where Isla sat opposite Aria and the cyborg. She was still watching him, her expression veiled. However, when their gazes met, something deep inside his chest tensed.

Shoving aside the discomforting sensation, Elijah glanced then at the girl seated next to Isla. With her black hair and pale skin, it was obvious that this was Isla's daughter, Beatrix. Unlike her mother, whose black hair was long and straight, the girl's mane was a riot of unruly curls.

Beatrix stared at him intently, her expression a blend of wariness and curiosity. And then, to his surprise, she asked, "Did my mother really try to kill you?"

"Bea!" Isla muttered. "That's not—"

"It's okay," Elijah replied, smiling. "I'll answer." He met Beatrix's eye once more then. "Yes, she did … more than once too … but we're friends now." He paused, his gaze flicking up to meet Isla's. "Aren't we?"

Isla's nostrils flared, high spots of color appearing on her cheeks. "The Mir-Ferrin clan-lord needs our help, Bea," she said softly. "That's why he's here."

"What kind of help?" There was a coolness to Beatrix's voice that hinted all wasn't well between mother and daughter. Indeed, the girl hadn't looked Isla's way once since taking a seat at the table.

"Bea—" It was Jenna this time who spoke up, but Elijah waved her warning away. "My younger brother has seized power," he told the girl. "And I want it back."

Malik snorted at this blunt, yet honest, response. "Of course, you do," he murmured.

Elijah didn't look his way. Instead, he remained focused on Bea. "I'm also here to see if I can repair things between our clans … before it's too late."

Bea's blue eyes, the same hue as her mother's, glinted. "I don't understand why Auntie Jen would want to talk to you … after what your family did to ours."

"She has no reason to," Elijah admitted. "Yet I have to ask, all the same."

Serving-droids were now bringing around steaming platters of food, yet no one paid the dinner any attention. Instead, Jenna cleared her throat. "We'll discuss the details of what peace between our clans *might* look like tomorrow, Mir-Ferrin." Her voice was clipped. "But for now, I'm interested in hearing what exactly you want from us in terms of help." She paused then, her expression hardening. "I'll warn you right now, we're not going to war on your behalf."

Elijah picked up the flute of sparkling wine in front of him and took a sip. "I'm not asking for that." And he wouldn't be. He'd been anticipating this question, and while he was showering and changing in his quarters he'd come up with an answer. However, he hadn't expected her to ask him this evening. "I need your assistance to locate one of my battleships, *Conqueror*. It's commanded by Grav Mir-Ferrin. He's someone I trust."

Jenna's brow furrowed. "And that's it?" She didn't bother to hide her suspicion.

"You'll need inside intel to locate the ship," Elijah pointed out. "So, before pulling your agents from Mir-Ferrin territory, I suggest you give them one last task."

Malik muttered something under his breath at this, while Jenna's delicate features tensed.

Of course, the subject of the eyes they *both* had in each other's territory had already been raised. However, Elijah's request that they use one of their agents to help him clearly rankled.

Meanwhile, Isla inclined her head, casting Elijah a searching look. Their gazes met for a moment before

Elijah leaned back in his seat and shifted his attention back to the clan-lady. "Your agents won't be put in any danger," he reassured her. "But since I no longer have my wrist-comm or tablet, I can't contact Commander Grav direct." It was true. The three dominant clans in the Rith Sector all used separate encrypted comms networks, isolated from the Public Sectornet which linked the rest of the sector, and the Shadownet, which was used primarily by the underworld. Direct lines could be opened between clan rulers, yet those channels wouldn't help Elijah at present.

There was no way the Mir-Brennan clan-lady could contact one of the Mir-Ferrin battleships direct, unless she was on one of her own battleships at close range.

"The only other thing I need is a small unmarked shuttle … no crew … it's best if I pilot it myself," Elijah added after a pause. "Once I know where *Conqueror* is, I shall set a course for it."

Silence followed these words.

Elijah took another sip of wine and waited for the clan-lady's response. He didn't think his requests were outlandish. However, they did require a level of trust—something he hadn't yet established with the Mir-Brennans.

"Once I take back my seat, I shall contact you," he assured Jenna when the silence drew out. "And we will begin to make our agreed-upon changes."

Lady Jenna sat back in her chair. "I have to say, I expected you to ask more of us than that."

Elijah shrugged. "That's all I need."

Her gaze narrowed, her fingers tightening around the stem of her glass. "Well then," she murmured. "We shall have to see."

"What *really* happened on Estradia?"

Glancing up, from where she'd been staring down into her drink, Isla met Jenna's eye.

The two women sat alone in a lounge in the clan-lady's quarters. Snug with over-stuffed sofas, nests of soft cushions, and floor-to-ceiling windows that looked over the illuminated cityscape beyond, it was a comfortable, relaxing space.

After a tension-filled dinner, it was a relief to retreat. However, Jenna's question caught Isla off-guard. Raising her glass to her lips, she took a gulp of pungent amber liquid. "I already told you."

"You've recounted *some* of what happened," Jenna replied. "Yet I have the distinct impression you've left quite a few details out."

Isla shifted uncomfortably on the sofa.

"You've slept with him, haven't you?"

It was hard not to flinch.

Isla hadn't said a word about what had passed between her and Elijah to anyone. But all the same, Jenna knew. Female instinct was rarely wrong about such things.

Silence fell in the lounge, swelling between them. Isla knew her lack of response was damning, yet she didn't know how to answer.

"For the love of the Gods, wipe that guilty look off your face," Jenna muttered. "I'm not going to condemn you."

Isla jolted, her gaze narrowing. "You aren't?"

She wasn't sure she'd have shown that much grace if their positions had been reversed.

"No … although I do question your taste."

Isla took another gulp of her drink. "Yeah, well … I'd rather not dwell on it." She paused then, dragging a hand through her hair. "If Bea ever found out, she'd never speak to me again."

"Really?" Jenna raised an eyebrow. "I think you underestimate your daughter."

Isla shook her head. "She's barely spoken to me since I arrived back, Jen."

"You only just got here … give it some time. She's just hurt, that's all." Jenna shook her head ruefully then. "She's proud and stubborn, like her mother."

Isla winced once more. She then set aside her glass and leaned back, raising her gaze to the spider-vaulted ceiling. "I made a terrible mistake, didn't I?"

Silence followed this comment before Jenna huffed a sigh. "No," she murmured. "You just used anger as a shield … to protect yourself from your grief."

Isla's throat constricted, tears stinging her eyelids. Blinking rapidly, she lowered her chin, her gaze meeting Jenna's. "That's what Mir-Ferrin said," she said huskily. "I didn't want to hear it at the time … but you're both right."

Jenna reached forward across the narrow space that separated them, her hand catching Isla's "I know how much you loved Cathal … and what losing him did to you." Her fingers tightened around Isla's. "But now you need to let yourself mourn him, Isla … it's time."

24. OUT FOR BLOOD

"WOULD YOU LIKE me to read you a bedtime story?"

"I'm too old for that, Ma."

Isla stiffened, putting down the tablet she'd just picked up from the table. "You're only nine," she pointed out wearily. "I still liked to hear bedtime stories at your age."

Her daughter's blue eyes narrowed, her jaw clenching.

They both knew the comment was a ruse though; Bea had a thirst for adventure and loved to hear about others traveling the galaxy.

Indeed, she'd just been on the edge of her seat, listening to Aria and Vic's news.

Two days had passed since Isla's return home, and their friends had stopped by after dinner. They'd just announced that they'd both given notices at their jobs. They'd bought themselves a freighter and would be departing Staturine II within the next fortnight.

The announcement came as a surprise to Isla. Of course, before leaving on her mission, she'd been so preoccupied that she'd barely noticed anyone else.

But now that she'd had time to think it over, their decision made sense.

Before he and Aria had gotten together, Vic had traveled the sector's trade routes with his battle-droid companion, Obsidian. He had a restless soul, and Aria shared his need for freedom.

After their friends had departed, leaving mother and daughter alone, Bea had sat on the sofa in their living area, her face mournful. Isla had thought a bedtime story might cheer her up, but her daughter still hadn't forgiven her, it seemed.

Holding Bea's gaze, Isla smiled. "I'm sure I can find you a tale about a brave girl who stows away on a space freighter."

Bea pulled a face, although her gaze glinted. "I don't want Aria to go away," she muttered. "Or Vic."

A pressure rose under Isla's breastbone. "I'll miss them too," she admitted.

Bea's throat bobbed then. "Everyone leaves," she whispered.

Isla moved across to her daughter, lowering herself down onto the sofa next to her. "Not everyone, love. I'm here."

Silence fell, stretching out as rain pattered on the large windows that surrounded them. Beyond, a murky dusk settled over Briscay. Finally, when Bea spoke, her voice trembled. "I know it's been a while … but I still miss dad."

Isla's chest started to ache. Suddenly, it was as if a tide were rising inside her, one she couldn't have stopped, even if she'd tried. "So do I," she whispered. She swallowed then as tears escaped, trickling down her face. She didn't bother to brush them away. "I didn't want to accept that he's gone … I tried to fight the Gods over it … but it was always a battle I was going to lose. I'm sorry I haven't been here for you, Bea. I neglected you, and then I left … I wasn't here when you needed me."

Her daughter's slender shoulders started to shake, and Isla realized she too was crying. Gently, she wrapped her arms around Bea. With a sob, her daughter buried her face in Isla's shoulder—and then, together, they wept.

Isla entered the clan-lady's solar and halted, her gaze sweeping the wide, window-lined space.

It was late afternoon, and Jenna had called an unscheduled meeting.

And despite that she'd told herself she wouldn't look his way immediately, Isla's gaze traveled straight to Elijah Mir-Ferrin.

She hadn't seen him in nearly four days. During that time, he'd been locked in negotiations with the clan-lady. Jenna hadn't invited him to dinner in the meantime either—something that had come as both a relief and a disappointment to Isla.

A relief because time apart from Elijah allowed her to focus on her daughter and gave her the chance to heal the grief they both shared—and disappointment because, although she constantly tried to convince herself otherwise, she found herself missing his company.

She'd rationalized her response by telling herself that since they'd been stuck together for days on Estradia, she had gotten used to having the man around.

However, deep down, she knew there was more to it than that.

Dressed in dark grey, his black hair swept back and tied at his nape, Elijah was rakishly handsome this afternoon, even if there were signs of strain around his mouth and eyes. After days of talks, he looked drained.

Isla was sure Jenna would have fought him on everything.

Across the room, Elijah's gaze met hers, and his mouth curved.

And Isla found herself smiling back.

Jenna cleared her throat then and rose from where she'd been seated behind her desk. Clad in flowing gold, the clan-lady swept out into the center of the solar, her gaze traveling around the faces of those she'd called to her: Malik, Aria, Vic, Elijah, and Isla.

"Two things," she said, her manner brisk. "The first is that Mir-Ferrin and I have finally drafted and signed a treaty."

"I thought we were announcing that tomorrow?" Malik murmured.

Jenna's features tightened. "Change of plans." Her attention then shifted to Elijah. "We found *Conqueror*."

"That was fast work," he replied, inclining his head.

"Not really … it was easy enough to find. The battleship is still orbiting Estradia." Jenna's brow furrowed then. "There appears to have been a coup on the planet … a group of extremists managed to storm the governor's residence three days ago. The Mir-Ferrins are in the process of trying to re-establish control."

Elijah's face tensed. "It sounds as if Grav has his hands full … I need to reach him."

Jenna favored him with a curt nod. "But that's not all … I take it none of you have watched this afternoon's news-reel?"

They all shook their heads.

"Well, the breaking story is that your brother has just claimed the Velix System as 'Mir-Ferrin' territory. He's seized control of its planets and put up a blockade, preventing our ships from entering."

Elijah's dark brows crashed together. "What? He hasn't even been sworn in as clan-lord yet."

"He's clearly eager to make a name for himself first," Jenna replied, her brow furrowing.

Likewise, Isla frowned. That was bad news. The Velix System has always been a buffer zone—sitting at the intersection between the Mir-Ferrin, Mir-Brennan, and Mir-Lelith territories.

"He's just broadcast a speech, in which he blames the Mir-Brennans for the destruction of *Defiance*," Jenna muttered. "He then announced that 'such a cold-blooded, unprovoked attack cannot go unpunished' … and that Mir-Brennan allies should question their allegiance."

"Of course, he did, My Lady," Vic said, his voice clipped. The cyborg folded his arms across his chest. "He's trying to draw you back into open conflict."

"I agree," Elijah replied. "That's exactly what he's doing."

"But won't the Mir-Leliths be angry about this too?" Aria asked, her face stern. "Surely, Lucas doesn't want to go to war with you both?"

"Lucas hasn't blocked Mir-Lelith ships from entering the Velix System … only ours," Jenna replied. "Vic is right … this move is aimed at antagonizing us."

Elijah muttered a curse under his breath. "He's out for blood … and he won't stop until he draws it." His attention cut back to Jenna then. "I need to get to Estradia and board *Conqueror*. Lucas can't stay in charge."

"On that, you'll get no argument," the clan-lady replied. "We're preparing a ship for you … it should be ready by the morning."

It was late. Isla should have been in bed, asleep—yet she wasn't.

Instead, she was pacing the deserted hallways of Valnor Castle.

He's leaving in the morning.

The knots in Isla's belly tightened. Gods, what did she care?

And yet she did.

In a few hours, Elijah would board that shuttle and disappear from her life forever. And it was the way things needed to be. There could never be anything between them; he was the Mir-Ferrin clan-lord, and she was the widow of the man they'd brought down.

Her connection with him was inappropriate, yet tonight, she didn't care.

After dinner, she and Bea had retired to their quarters. They'd then watched a vid together, curled up on the sofa. Bea had gone to bed afterward, while Isla remained in the lounge.

Alone, she'd sat, staring out the wide windows, wrestling with her thoughts. She should have retired too, but instead, she'd taken a walk.

And that walk had led her straight to Elijah's door.

The rest of the castle slept, save those members of the Watch patrolling the empty corridors and courtyards of the vast fortress. Yet Isla was alone in this wing. Approaching the guest room that he'd been allotted, she was surprised not to see guards flanking the entrance.

Since Elijah's arrival, Jenna had ensured two of her Watch always shadowed him—but tonight, she'd left none of her security team to watch over him.

It was a gesture of trust.

Jenna Mir-Brennan and Elijah Mir-Ferrin weren't likely ever to be friends, but the past days of negotiations had built a grudging respect. Isla had noted a change in Jenna's manner when she addressed Elijah earlier. They'd locked horns for days, but in the end, they'd agreed upon the treaty they'd both signed.

Breathing shallowly, Isla halted before Elijah's door and pressed the comm next to it.

Silence followed, and she waited in the hallway, her pulse fluttering in her throat now.

Maybe he was in a deep sleep.

Doubt crept in then, and she swallowed, cursing her impulsive behavior. This was the man she'd once sworn to kill—she shouldn't be drawn to his door.

And yet she was.

I shouldn't disturb him.

She stepped back, planning to retrace her steps and retreat to her quarters.

However, the door whispered open.

Elijah stood there. Naked to the waist, he wore loose pants with a draw-string waist that sat low on his hips. His dark hair was mussed, and he blinked sleepily as his gaze settled upon her. "Isla." The rumble of his voice sent a ripple of awareness through her. "What are you doing here?"

Isla managed a tight, nervous smile. "I couldn't sleep," she murmured, "not without saying goodbye first." She broke off then, warmth rising to her face. Gods, she wished her voice didn't sound so breathy. This wasn't good at all. She took another step back. "I'm sorry … I've woken you up. I should go."

25. IF I WERE SOMEONE ELSE

HANDS CLENCHING AT her sides, Isla turned—but Elijah forestalled her. "Don't apologize … I wanted to see you too."

Isla froze. "You did?"

A slow smile spread across his face as the remnants of sleep faded from his dark gaze. "Yes … do you want to come in?"

Isla swallowed before nodding silently.

Elijah stepped back, allowing her to enter his bedchamber. As the door whispered closed, he headed toward the nearby sideboard, where a row of cut-glass tumblers and a carafe of amber-colored liquid sat. "I'm going to have a nectini brandy," he announced. "Do you want one?"

"Yes … thanks," Isla replied. In truth, she needed something to settle her nerves.

She'd never felt so unsure of herself.

Glancing around, she realized that Jenna had given him one of the largest and most luxurious guest rooms: everything was white and gold. Plush white mats covered a polished golden floor. A huge, canopied bed sat at the far end of the rectangular space, while at the other end, with a majestic view over Briscay's twinkling skyline, was a long sofa and two armchairs.

It was a lovely suite, but Elijah was a clan-lord, after all.

Isla moved over to the large window and stood looking out at the view while Elijah poured them two small tumblers. He handed Isla her glass and then met her eye as he held up his tumbler in a toast. "To putting things right," he murmured.

"Yes," she replied huskily. "Let's drink to that."

Their glasses clinked, and then they raised their tumblers to their lips and sipped. Liquid fire flowed down Isla's throat, igniting in the pit of her belly. "That's good," she sighed. "I've never felt at home on this planet ... but they do make good brandy."

"I heard nectini fruit only grow here."

Isla nodded. "It's the minerals in the soil."

She lapsed into silence then, and raised her glass to her lips once more, taking a bigger sip this time. Dammit, she hadn't visited Elijah to talk about the local brandy.

Her breathing hitched. *Why are you here then?*

She tightened her grip on her glass as if it was her anchor, while she struggled to think of something to say that wouldn't make her sound like an idiot.

Elijah saved her.

"Things have been ... intense ... over the past days," he said softly. "We haven't had the chance to see each other, let alone talk."

Isla's already racing heart increased speed. "I thought you'd be relieved to be free of me," she replied. "After ... everything that's happened."

Their gazes fused then before he replied, "Well, you're mistaken."

Isla concentrated on keeping her breathing slow and even, for she was keenly aware that he was half-naked. Those pants hung so low on his hips that she could see where his stomach muscles arrowed down to his—

Gods, she shouldn't stare at him like that. Isla's gaze snapped up, and she found him watching her.

A slight smile played on his lips, one tinged with masculine arrogance. A week ago, such a smile would have made her want to bury her fist in his face, but tonight, it caused desire to hammer against her breastbone.

The air between them suddenly felt heavy.

"It's strange how things work out." Elijah stepped forward so that they now stood little more than three feet apart. "You were rabid when we met, but once we reached Scull Basin, things changed between us." His smile had faded now, his dark eyes spearing her. "I've never felt so comfortable with anyone. It's like I could tell you anything and you'd listen."

Isla swallowed. "I'm not sure how I feel about being called 'rabid'."

"Well, you did try to kill me multiple times." He paused then and moved closer still. And then, to her surprise, he lifted a hand and gently brushed her cheek with the back of his fingers.

And to Isla's even greater surprise, she trembled under his touch.

"Sorry, Isla," he said, his voice husky now. "I'm not practiced at this … I'm rarely at a loss for words in political negotiations, but with you, I'm a lot less sure of myself."

He stroked her cheek once more, and Isla's breathing hitched. There it was again, that same hunger that had swept her away that night back in Crelcaster. Without even realizing what she was doing, she swayed toward him, yet she checked the instinct to lose control.

She wanted to stay in the present.

Elijah inhaled sharply. "What I'm trying to say," he continued. "Is that I've never truly let my guard down with anyone … until I spent time with you." The pad of his thumb swept across her lower lip then, and when he continued, his voice lowered further. "You don't give a shit what I think of you … but I find that I want you to like me."

Despite that it was hard to concentrate with his sensual caress moving down her jawline to her throat now, Isla managed to answer. "You're wrong, Elijah," she whispered. "I do care … why do you think I'm here?"

Elijah's trailing fingertips left her throat then, and he took her half-finished tumbler of brandy from her. He placed the glasses on the low table behind them and returned to her. This time, he gently grasped her wrist and, turning it over, raised it to his lips.

Dizziness swept over Isla at the gentle brush of his mouth against her racing pulse.

"If I were someone else, you could have been mine, Isla," he murmured against the sensitive skin of her wrist. "But there are too many strikes against us."

Isla's throat constricted. "There are." They both knew it, and yet she'd come to him anyway. "This time tomorrow, you'll be in hyperspace, traveling to Estradia … but right now, you're here … and so am I." She broke off then, her free hand rising to caress the strong line of his jaw as he still bent his head to her wrist. "We have a few hours … let's make them count."

Elijah straightened up and, still holding her wrist, drew her against him.

And when he lowered his head to claim her mouth, Isla fell into him.

A heartbeat later, they were kissing feverishly.

Isla wrapped her arms around his neck, drawing him close, her tongue sliding against his.

Elijah tasted of the sweet, fruity brandy with a hint of citrus. Yet he smelled fresh, like a winter's dawn on this planet, and the soap he'd used to bathe left the scent of conifers on his skin.

Isla's eyes fluttered closed, and she drank him in, her body melting against his.

Elijah groaned low in his throat as he kissed her, his hands tunneling through her hair, his fingertips splaying across the back of her head. He deepened the kiss— and a moment later, Isla found her back pressed up against cold glass.

His mouth left hers then, trailing down her jaw, to her throat. "This dress," he murmured. "It was hard not to stare when you turned up at the meeting earlier… all I could think about was peeling it off you."

Isla blinked, trying to focus. She'd forgotten she was wearing the same figure-hugging dark-blue tunic as earlier. Truthfully, when she'd left her quarters, and roamed the hallways of the castle, she'd been too distracted to pay attention to her outfit.

But Elijah had.

He found the fastenings on the back, and a second later, he really was peeling off her dress.

Isla was in full view of the window here, although they were so high up that no one—unless they had binoculars trained on them—could see her right now.

She couldn't care less if anyone saw them though. All she could think about, all she could focus on, was the man she was with.

The air breathed over her naked skin as Elijah pushed the dress down over her hips and let it ripple to the floor. He then unfastened her bra and tossed it aside before his fingers hooked over the silky edges of her panties and pushed them down. He then stepped back, his gaze raking over her naked body.

"Gods," he whispered. "Look at you."

Heat flushed across Isla's chest, and she started to breathe fast. Her bare breasts jutted shamelessly up at him, her nipples aching to be touched, while excitement fluttered through her body. "I want to see you too," she said huskily.

Holding her eye, he undid the drawstring on his pants and then dropped them.

Isla's lips parted as she let her gaze slide down over the sculpted muscles of his chest and torso, to where his cock thrust up against his stomach, rigid and thick. Its swollen tip was slick—and moving on instinct, Isla sank to her knees before him.

Need pulsed between her thighs, hunger twisting inside her.

She wanted—*needed*—to taste him.

Elijah groaned as she cupped his balls with one hand and wrapped her fingers around the base of his shaft with her other. Then, leaning in, she took him as deep as she could into her mouth.

Elijah gasped a curse, arching against her, his hands tangling in her hair while she worked him, sucking, stroking, and licking. "Isla," he groaned before muttering something intelligible.

Isla responded by flicking her tongue along the sensitive underside of the head of his shaft.

Elijah made a strangled sound and jerked back from her. "Not yet," he gasped.

Reaching down, he pulled her to her feet and pushed her back up against the window. The next moment, he was hungrily kissing his way down her body.

Isla writhed against the cold glass as he suckled each breast until she gasped, until she whimpered.

Sinking to the ground before her, he pushed her trembling thighs apart, took hold of one leg, and slung it over his shoulder. He then spread her wide for him.

And when his mouth found her, Isla's raw cry echoed through the bedchamber. She bucked against him, her hands tangling in his hair as she urged him on.

Elijah didn't seem to need any encouragement though—and he knew just where to lick, where to flick the tip of his tongue.

Before Isla knew what she was doing, her legs started to twitch and jerk, and a wave of delicious pleasure exploded between her thighs, pulsing through her womb. If he hadn't been holding her, pinned against the window, she'd have collapsed.

But Elijah wasn't finished. He suckled her then, hard, like he had her nipples, and another spasm of ecstasy crashed into her.

Isla writhed against him, gasping his name.

She thought he might take her there, might turn her to the window and plunge into her from behind. Hunger twisted hard in her core as she imagined it.

Yet, instead, Elijah rose to his feet and scooped her into his arms.

Isla—still shaking from her climax, her limbs boneless—collapsed against the hard wall of his chest, while he carried her away from the window to the bed.

He laid her out there, upon cool sheets, before he crawled over her.

Then, husking her name once more, Elijah claimed her mouth with his.

The feel of his tongue tangling with hers, of his hands sliding over her sweat-damp skin, was overwhelming.

Within seconds, Isla was lost.

She spread her thighs for him and wrapped her legs around his hips, trying to pull him into her.

Gods, she wanted him.

Groaning a curse, he fisted himself and positioned the glistening head of his cock at her entrance—and then he slammed deep into her.

Isla cried out, spreading her thighs wide to accommodate him. Her fingernails raked his back while her ankles locked around his hips, and she pulled him in deeper still.

He took her hard, in punishing thrusts.

Their first time together, he'd let her take control, yet this time, he was dominant, fierce.

And how she loved it. She could never get enough of it.

The rasp of their breathing, her whimpers and his groans of pleasure, and the slap of their flesh colliding, filled the room.

Isla could feel another climax building, curling in her lower belly, and she clawed her way toward it.

Writhing against Elijah, she gasped his name once more.

Sensing her urgency, he changed position, pushing her legs up so her thighs pressed against her belly. He then grasped her hips and yanked them up to meet his with every bold stroke.

Isla unraveled.

Sobbing, she arched back while she ground her pelvis into his, wild, wet pleasure twisting through her. This was too much, too intense—yet it was incredible.

An instant later, Elijah's hoarse cry joined her sobs, and the powerful heat of his release filled her.

26. THINGS THAT COULD NEVER BE

IT WAS OVER.

Breathing hard, their bodies slick with sweat, they clung to each other without speaking for a long while.

Eventually, when Elijah raised his face from where it had been buried in the curve of her shoulder, his eyes glittered.

Isla's throat constricted.

Jidea, she hadn't expected him to ever look at her like that.

His gaze was raw, naked, vulnerable—and it made her feel things she shouldn't. Things that could never be.

Swallowing the painful lump in her throat, she raised a trembling hand and stroked his cheek. "Elijah," she whispered. "I don't—"

"It's okay," he replied huskily, cupping his hand over hers. "I'll be right in a minute or two." He paused then. "I got carried away … I didn't hurt you, did I?"

"No," she murmured. It was true, he hadn't. "You gave me exactly what I wanted."

His dark-brown eyes deepened to ebony as he stared down at her. The seconds ticked by, and then he inhaled deeply. "I never expected to have time alone with you again."

"Neither did I." She held his gaze, even as the tightness in her throat spread to her chest. "But I couldn't let you leave" —she managed a wobbly smile then— "Not without a *proper* goodbye."

Elijah's mouth, swollen from the violence of their kisses, lifted at the corners. "Isla Mir-Brennan," he murmured her name in a caress. "Once my bane … and now …" His voice trailed off, his expression turning wry. "I'm not sure exactly *what* you are now."

She huffed a soft laugh. "Let's say I'm unclassifiable … and leave it at that."

His smile widened. "You certainly are."

Elijah halted at the edge of the landing pad and surveyed the battered freighter waiting for him.

This wasn't the shuttle he'd been promised.

Turning, his gaze traveled over the small party that had come down to see him off: Lady Jenna, Malik, Vic, and Aria—and Isla and Bea.

"Where did you get *that?*" he asked, his attention resting upon the clan-lady.

"It's space-worthy," Vic replied before Jenna could speak. "The engine's solid, even if the fuselage is a bit banged up." He paused then, and Elijah swore he saw the cyborg's single eye glint. "And even unmarked—a Mir-Brennan shuttle is easy to identify. A Mir-Ferrin freighter will raise fewer suspicions."

"My captain is right," Jenna said then, a slight smile upon her lips. "If you want to approach one of your battleships without being shot down, best you look as unthreatening as possible."

Elijah's lips pursed. As much as it galled him to admit it, they both had a point. Even so, when he glanced back at the ship, he frowned. He now wished he hadn't let Greta Mir-Hamil depart. Although the *CS Intrepid* was a D-class freighter like this one, her ship had been in much better condition. This freighter's shields were dented and carbon-scored, as if it had seen recent action.

"It's called *The Stalwart*," Malik added then, not bothering to hide the smug edge to his voice.

Elijah deliberately kept his gaze upon his new ship, even as his jaw tensed.

Damn them all—they were all having a bit of fun at his expense.

"Can you actually fly it?" Bea asked then.

Aria made a choking sound that sounded like a smothered laugh, and Elijah turned to find most of the group behind him either smirking or trying to hide it.

However, unlike on the first occasion they'd met, there was no hostility in Bea's manner this morning.

"Yes," he replied, meeting her eye. "I learned to fly as a teenager." His mouth twitched then. "Not even clan-lord's sons escape military service."

Especially not a Mir-Ferrin clan-lord's son, he silently added. His father had insisted all three of his sons learned how to handle themselves in a fight and how to fly Arrows and shuttles.

"The ship's papers are all in order," Jenna informed him then. The clan-lady's expression had sobered. She'd no doubt remembered that his safe return to his clan was serious business. If he didn't deal with Lucas, and soon, they were *all* in trouble. "You're Captain Eral Mir-Ferrin, traveling from Cadex 12 to Estradia with a shipment of mining machinery." She paused then. "Just in case they check your nav-log ... I suggest making a stop at Cadex 12 en route, and refueling there, before continuing to Estradia."

Elijah nodded, relaxing his jaw just a little. That made sense.

"Here ... you'll need this." Isla moved forward, holding out a small circular device that gleamed dully in the overhead lights inside the hangar. "The PCSD has two thousand credits on it."

Their fingers brushed as she handed him the device, and Elijah's pulse kicked up a notch.

Struggling to focus, he nodded before slipping the PCSD into the thigh pocket of the cargo pants he wore. "Thank you." He then shifted his attention back to the clan-lady.

Jenna was watching him intently, a glint in her eye.

Elijah's heart kicked against his ribs as he realized that, somehow, she knew about him and Isla.

He looked over the faces of the small party flanking the clan-lady, and his pulse quickened further.

Bea was still staring up at him, curiosity imprinted on her young face. However, the expressions of the others were all shuttered, their gazes sharp.

They all know.

Resisting the urge to glance Isla's way, to shoot her a questioning look, Elijah drew in a slow, steadying breath.

Isla was too private to have said anything, yet the clan-lady would have security cams all over the fortress. Of course, they'd have spotted Isla entering his quarters.

But it was too late to worry about such things now—and he meant what he'd told Isla back on Estradia after they'd slept together for the first time.

He had no regrets. None regarding what they'd done, anyway—only that he hadn't been born into a different family.

Elijah inhaled deeply before announcing, "Right then … I'll be off." He shifted his attention to Jenna, holding her gaze. "As soon as I re-establish control on Platinum 5, I will open a channel to you," he assured her. "And if you don't hear from me, it's because I've failed."

Silence followed these words—for they were a reminder of what was at stake.

Jenna nodded. "You *won't* fail," she replied firmly. "I'll be waiting for your call."

Elijah nodded back. He then glanced over at Isla. After handing him the PCSD, she hadn't returned to the group. Instead, she stood at his side. Her expression was unreadable though. "Can we have a minute or two alone?" he murmured.

Their gazes held before she nodded. "Okay." Isla then waved the others off. "Go on … I'll join you all shortly."

None of them looked pleased to be dismissed. Bea flashed him a penetrating look that reminded him of her mother, while Jenna's features tightened. Malik was frowning, and Vic's broad shoulders had gone rigid.

Beside the cyborg, Aria's emerald gaze flicked between Elijah and Isla.

Nonetheless, they all departed—and when they did, Elijah favored Isla with a half-smile. "Well, I guess the secret's out."

Isla sighed. "If it wasn't before … it *is* now."

Their gazes held before he asked, "Do you care?"

"I did," she murmured. "But not anymore."

Elijah stepped close then, and she raised her chin to hold his eye. Her nearness brought back images of the night before.

His breathing caught as the truth settled on him.

This woman was *everything*.

"You probably don't want to hear his name on my lips … but although Cathal's life was cut short, I envy him," he said softly. Isla's eyes snapped wide, a muscle feathering in her jaw, yet he continued. He had to say this before his courage deserted him. "He had years with you … he had your love … but all I'll be left with is memories." He swallowed hard. "And maybe that's all I deserve."

He stopped there; he had to. Elijah wasn't used to dealing with such strong emotions. He felt out of control, while at the same time calmer and surer of himself than he'd ever been. He stepped in closer still, cupping her face with his hands. Isla trembled under his touch, and her reaction emboldened him to continue. "It's an impossible dream, but I'm going to say it anyway. If you want it, there's a place for you at my side … as my wife."

Isla went rigid against him. She stopped breathing, her lips parting in shock. "What—"

"And there's a place for Beatrix too," he went on, his voice catching as nervousness barreled into him. He was making a fool of himself, yet he didn't care. He had to say this. He couldn't leave without Isla knowing. "For *both* of you."

He broke off then, his heart slamming painfully against his breastbone. It really was impossible, he knew it, but there was no taking those words back.

He had to face the truth. Whatever this had been between them, it was coming to an end.

Elijah gently traced the lush curve of her lower lip with his thumb. His chest ached now. "You deserve to be loved, to be cherished," he said softly. "I want you to be happy, Isla, even if that means I can never have you. Promise me, you'll make a new start … that you'll leave the pain, the bitterness, behind you."

She stared up at him, her dark-blue eyes gleaming now. A lengthy pause drew out, before she whispered, "I will … but make me a promise too, Elijah." She reached up then, her fingers curling around his wrist. "When you return to Platinum 5, when you retake your seat, don't doubt yourself again. You're a man with compassion, with a fair and just heart. And you instinctively understand what it takes to rule well. That's not weakness, that's what true strength is … so embrace who you are."

Elijah's breathing grew shallow. No one had ever said anything like that to him before—had ever believed in him so vehemently—and he didn't know how to respond. Even so, his chest ached cruelly now. Their gaze drew out before he eventually nodded. "I will," he said thickly. He leaned in, his lips teasing hers in a gentle, tender kiss. He then drew back, dropping his hands from her cheeks. "Goodbye, Isla."

She released his wrist, her hands falling to her sides before whispering, "Goodbye."

He turned on his heel, blinking as his vision blurred, and climbed the metal stairs to the landing pad. Without a backward glance, he strode over to the waiting freighter, ascending the ramp into its belly.

Slamming his fist on the panel by the door and letting the hatch rise, sealing him inside, Elijah stood there a moment, jaw clenched, blinking rapidly.

Enough. He needed to pull himself together.

27. IT'S TIME

ISLA MOVED BACK from the landing pad, watching as *The Stalwart's* engines thrummed into life. Their power made the floor beneath her feet vibrate. As she waited, the engines rose to a whine, and the ship lifted off the pad, rotating slowly away from her.

Her attention remained fixed upon it.

She couldn't see Elijah at the controls, for the cockpit window was facing toward the hangar doors now.

And it was just as well, for tears trickled down her cheeks.

There was no one present to see. Not that she focused on that. It was taking everything she had not to run after him, not to beg him to take her and Bea with him.

Luckily, she was sane enough to realize that to do so was madness. All the same, the pain in her throat revealed that she cared far more for Elijah Mir-Ferrin than she should have.

His honesty had shocked her, yet even as he'd offered to marry her, to have her at his side, she'd seen the bleakness in his eyes.

He knew the truth of it, as she did.

Some things were impossible.

She'd meant what she'd told him though—she knew his worth, and she couldn't let him leave without telling him.

The Stalwart moved toward the hangar doors, the engines increasing in pitch. Isla shouldn't really have been standing this close without ear protectors, and so she backed off, placing her hands over her ears.

Vic was right—although the freighter looked as if it had just been in a skirmish, there didn't sound as if there was anything wrong with those powerful engines.

It would get him safely to his destination.

The Stalwart's rear thrusters engaged then, bright white light flaring, and the freighter shot forward, arrowing out of the hangar into the dawn-brushed sky beyond.

Isla watched Elijah go. Her tears were close to blinding her now, and she scrubbed at her eyes.

She needed to regain control before she emerged from the hangar—before she faced her family again.

Her time with Elijah had turned her world on its axis. It had taught her that people, or situations, were rarely as straightforward as they first seemed. And it had released her from the prison of her own hate.

She felt pummeled right now, yet she was lighter too.

Isla could be a proper mother to Bea once more. She could make plans without having to contend with a gnawing unrest in her gut, without fury clouding everything.

She smiled then, her gaze lingering on where the freighter had disappeared to a pinprick on the horizon.

It was ironic that, despite it all, she had much to thank Elijah Mir-Ferrin for.

By the time Elijah brought *The Stalwart* out of hyperspace for the second time on the journey, and he spied the sleek silver bulk of *Conqueror* orbiting Estradia, he was ready for action.

Vic hadn't been lying; the ship might have looked as if it was going to fall to pieces, yet it handled beautifully, and its engines purred as it slid back into light, and then cruise, speed.

Seated in the cockpit, Elijah heaved in a deep breath and leaned forward, punching the comm. He then slid a finger across the display, altering the frequency so that he didn't connect with Tower Control at Crelcaster but with the battlecruiser he now approached.

"Here goes," he murmured.

The comm crackled into life. "Unidentified D-class freighter, please identify yourself," a comms-officer barked.

"Apologies, *Conqueror*," Elijah greeted the officer, careful to keep his tone low and respectful. "Captain Eral Mir-Ferrin of *The Stalwart* here. I'm bound for Crelcaster spaceport with a shipment of mining machinery, but I've run into some mechanical trouble. My ship's landing gear has jammed … permission requested to land onboard your ship and fix the problem." He paused there and cleared his throat, as if embarrassed. "Sorry for the inconvenience."

During the journey here, Elijah had gone through a few different ways to approach this. He'd considered asking to speak to Commander Grav direct but was concerned the comms-officer would refuse him.

And judging from this one's greeting, he would have.

"Captain, you do realize Crelcaster spaceport is closed at present," the comms-officer replied, a withering note creeping into his voice. "Riots are going on … and the capital is in lock-down."

"Really?" Elijah broke off then before muttering. "I knew I should've checked the news-reels before leaving Cadex 12. I didn't even—"

"Permission granted to board," the comms-officer cut him off, his patience fraying. "Approach the starboard side, and dock in landing bay 441X. We'll have a crew waiting to assist you."

"Copy," Elijah replied, injecting a relieved, cheery tone. "Thank you." The relief wasn't feigned. He'd spent nearly two days making this journey, slowed down by the necessity to make a stop at Cadex 12. During that time, thoughts of Isla had plagued him. The memory of her standing in that landing bay, her beautiful midnight-blue eyes gleaming, her face stricken, haunted him. But now he'd arrived at his destination, he was relieved to be able to act, to focus on his brother.

The Gods only knew what Lucas was up to now.

The comms-officer didn't bother to sign off; he merely cut the transmission.

Exhaling sharply, Elijah angled the freighter toward the massive battlecruiser.

"Convinced now?" Elijah inclined his head, fixing the security-officer with a steely look. He then removed his hand from the ID scanner the female Nandoon had just presented him with.

Staring down at the display, Ensign Lessa Mir-Barus's wattles quivered. "Apologies, *My Lord* … but we all believed you were dead." Her deep-set eyes were riveted upon his face, her expression stunned.

But Elijah wasn't a shade back from the dead.

He was the Mir-Ferrin clan-lord, and he was quickly losing patience.

They stood by a bank of elevators just beyond the landing bays. Elijah had called one of the elevators when Ensign Lessa had cornered him and refused to let him go any farther.

She was only doing her job, of course, with a zeal that he'd commend under other circumstances. But right now, impatience churned within him.

"Take me to Commander Grav," Elijah ordered. "I must speak to him urgently."

The officer's long proboscis twitched. "Of course, My Lord." The security-officer stepped away to call the nearest elevator. Clad in a bronze jumpsuit, the Nandoon was nearly as tall as him. She also carried a heavy weapon belt around her hips, where a laser-pistol and a laser-blade hung. Elijah had been wary of tangling with her. As such, he hadn't argued when she'd thrust the ID scanner at him.

He'd told her he was Elijah Mir-Ferrin, yet she wouldn't believe it until the scanner confirmed his DNA.

The ride up to the command deck was a tense one.

Lessa Mir-Barus kept cutting him nervous glances, as if she expected a reprisal for not believing him earlier. However, Elijah wasn't bothered about that—his thoughts were already shifting forward, to what needed to be done.

Commander Grav was standing on the bridge, talking to one of his officers, when Elijah followed the security-officer through the sliding doors. Tall and spare, Grav's long face went slack, and his pale-blue eyes snapped wide.

He then breathed a curse.

Likewise, the officers around him stared.

Elijah ignored everyone except the commander.

Warmth suffused Elijah's chest then; out of all his commanders, Grav was the one he could call a friend.

Grav Mir-Ferrin was earnest, serious, and a confirmed bachelor; he'd forgone all family ties for a glittering career.

Elijah moved around Ensign Lessa and strode to the commander, halting before him. He then smiled. "Didn't expect to ever see me again, did you, Grav?"

The commander swallowed. "My L … Lord," he stuttered. "How—"

"I'll elaborate on the details later," Elijah interrupted him. "But for now, you just need to know that my brother sabotaged *Defiance*. I was supposed to die along with the rest of my crew … but when I survived, he sent assassins down to Estradia to finish the job." Elijah paused there, aware that silence had fallen upon the bridge. He then flashed Grav another smile, although this one was humorless. "As you can see, they too failed."

A nerve flickered in the commander's cheek. "My Lord," he said roughly. "I had no idea, I swear."

"I know you didn't … I wouldn't have come to you otherwise." Elijah stepped closer to him. He then raised a hand and placed it firmly on Grav's shoulder. "Can I count on your loyalty, Commander?"

"Always, My Lord."

Elijah grinned. "Good … now … set a course for the Velix System. It's time we dealt with my brother."

The shadowy temple was a refuge from the rumble of the busy city just outside its doors.

Boots whispering on the large stone pavers covering the floor, Isla made her way toward the altar.

It was two days following Elijah's departure—and Cathal's birthday. And as she always had since Cathal's death, Isla made a morning visit to the Temple of Jidea to light a candle in his memory.

There weren't many people inside the temple at this hour—mid-morning—but Isla had chosen this time specifically. She didn't want distractions. Despite Briscay's size, this was the only temple to the Goddess of Fortune. The most celebrated gods on Staturine II were the Goddess Fara, and her sister, Nain.

But on Idral, where Isla's husband grew up, Jidea was revered.

The Goddess herself, robed and holding a great hammer aloft, rose above the altar and the circle of flickering candles. Cathal had often visited the temple at Melor, near Mir-Brennan Tower on Idral. He'd once told Isla that his faith in Jidea, mistress of fate, made it easier to rule.

He would have been thirty-six today.

Wordlessly, she helped herself to an unlit candle. She then lit it from those already burning, placing the candle at the center of the circular stand.

Isla's gaze settled upon the dancing golden flames. "Good morning, Cathal," she murmured. "It's been a while."

That was true: in the first months after his death, she'd visited this temple every couple of days. It made her feel closer to him, and the quiet soothed her.

The last time she'd stepped inside a Temple to Jidea had been on Idral; it had been just days before she set off on her hunt to kill the remaining two members of the Mir-Ferrin ruling family. On that day, she'd knelt before the altar and promised Cathal she'd take reckoning on his behalf.

She'd been filled with righteous anger after visiting the pile of ash that had once been Mir-Brennan Tower. And she'd growled her promise to the candle she'd lit.

Elijah and Lucas Mir-Ferrin would die by her hand.

"Things didn't exactly work out as planned, my love," she admitted then. "I set off to avenge you … but then ended up allying myself with Elijah Mir-Ferrin." She broke off, lowering herself to her knees before the altar. "I gave myself to him, twice. You probably wouldn't approve of my choice of lover … but you didn't ask me to carry all that hate with me, you didn't demand I seek reckoning for your death. I shouldered that burden all on my own." She blinked then as tears stung the back of her eyes. "You were a good man … you were my love, and I will always carry a part of you with me." She reached up with one hand and placed a clenched hand over her breastbone. "In my heart." She inhaled deeply as emotion swept over her. Without fail, she felt close to her dead husband here, and this morning was no exception. "But I realize now that I have to let the past go."

She fell silent then, head bent.

Around her, the emptiness was hollow, profound. Isla closed her eyes and allowed herself to soak it in, to let peace settle over her.

It had been a long while since she'd knelt in a Temple to Jidea without murder in her heart. The absence of anger felt strange; yet it was a reminder of how much she'd strayed, of how close she'd come to losing herself completely.

Eventually, her knees started to hurt. The pavers she knelt on were hard and cold.

Isla opened her eyes, her gaze resting on the flickering flame. Peace settled over her then, wrapping around her like a soft blanket, and she smiled.

It was as if Cathal were with her, telling her it was all right.

He understood.

Pushing herself to her feet, Isla dusted off her pants and favored the candle with another smile. "I'll say a prayer for your next birthday, I promise," she murmured. "And next time, I'll bring Bea." She nodded then to the statue of the Goddess that reared above her. "Jidea be praised."

28. AFTER YOU

"WE'RE ABOUT TO come out of hyperspace, My Lord."

"Thank you, Commander." Elijah buckled the empty laser-pistol holster around his hips. He was alone in his quarters and had just finished dressing in black body armor. "Have you readied your team?"

"Yes, My Lord. *Dominion* is orbiting Goliath 4. As soon as we do the same, we'll board a shuttle for the flagship." The commander's voice, which emitted from the new wrist-comm Elijah wore, halted. "Lucas is expecting me."

"Of course, he will be," Elijah murmured. "There are few things my brother likes better than a vigorous torture session. He won't be able to resist a visit to the detention area."

They'd come up with a good plan—one that would hopefully get Elijah onboard *Dominion* and face-to-face with his brother without being killed first. Grav had contacted Lucas to inform him that he'd arrested the leader of the *Creed of Truth* rebels in Crelcaster. They'd brought him up to *Conqueror* and interrogated him—in an attempt to discover the location of the other cells, and who led them—but the man had been remarkably resilient.

It was frustrating, for they still knew too little about the extremists.

Lucas had recently had a new interrogation suite installed on his flagship—with a specialist interrogator at his disposal. It was then no surprise when he insisted Grav bring his prisoner to the Velix System.

"Are you ready, My Lord?" Grav asked then.

"Yes … I'm on my way to join you now."

Elijah tapped his finger on his wrist-comm and reached for his helmet. It was black and covered his entire face. He'd put it on before he boarded *Dominion*.

Best to keep his face hidden until he had Lucas in front of him.

Leaving his quarters, Elijah strode along the brightly lit corridor beyond to the elevators. From there, he traveled down to the aft landing bays.

And as the elevator shot downward, Elijah reflected that his brother's aggressive move against the Mir-Brennans had actually been a blessing in disguise.

Lucas's arrogance had worked in his favor.

Once his brother returned to Platinum 5, once he was sworn officially in as clan-lord, he'd be much harder to displace. Not only that, but a guard of battle-droids patrolled Alpha Deck and the clan-lord's residence.

Of course, there would be battle-droids on his brother's flagship, but Grav would also be bringing his own team with him. If they moved fast, they'd be able to take control of the bridge once Lucas was arrested and reprogram the droids from there.

A short while later, Elijah strode into the landing bay to find Grav and his team waiting for him before a gleaming transport shuttle.

Flashing the commander a grin, Elijah halted before the group. His gaze then swept over the figures, standing rigidly to attention on either side of him. As he'd requested, the commander had a full security team with him that included six battle-droids and the same number of cyborgs. "Well done, Grav," he murmured.

Over the years, Grav had always been loyal to Elijah—and he'd now proved his trustworthiness once again.

The commander dipped his head, the corners of his mouth tilting in a slight smile. "After you, My Lord."

He stepped aside then, to let the clan-lord board the shuttle first.

Inside, Elijah took one of the seats in the middle of the central cabin and strapped himself in. Grav sat down behind him, while the rest of his team harnessed themselves against the walls.

Moments later, the shuttle's engines thrummed to life.

They slid out of *Conqueror,* bridging the distance between the two battlecruisers orbiting Goliath 4. The planet, the most heavily populated and prosperous in the buffer system, was the logical place for Lucas to take control.

Elijah's gaze remained fixed on the cockpit window ahead, where the two pilots perched, taking in the mauve, tan, and cream surface of the massive planet.

His breathing quickened then, determination hardening his stomach.

Lucas had always been the most impetuous of the three Mir-Ferrin brothers. Even their father wouldn't have rushed into conflict like this, not without preparing for it. After losing their battle against the Mir-Brennans to hold Idral, their space fleet had taken a significant hit—one they'd not yet recovered from.

Nonetheless, the Mir-Ferrins were still more powerful than those who ruled the peaceful Velix System.

Elijah's mouth thinned. His brother would have earned their clan new enemies with this act of aggression—something they didn't need, since their list of allies was already thin.

He had to regain control, and swiftly. He couldn't let himself consider the possibility of failure.

But as the sleek silver and bronze hull of *Dominion* loomed, becoming the heavens, Elijah remembered the *Defiance*, and the thousands of souls that had served upon it.

All dead. All gone.

His ribcage constricted.

Lucas had committed a terrible crime—and he'd pay for what he'd done.

Elijah's eyes flickered shut, and as he did so, his thoughts shifted to the woman he'd left behind. He shouldn't be thinking about Isla right now, yet ever since departing Staturine II, it had been a struggle to keep her out of his mind.

He couldn't help but feel a fool. He hadn't been planning to ask her to marry him. But as they'd stood together alone in that hangar, he'd been unable to stop himself.

All the same, he hadn't been surprised that she didn't jump at the chance.

There was no doubt there was something powerful between them—but it wasn't enough to smooth over the past.

An ache rose in Elijah's chest then. He knew all that, of course, and had spent the hours alone during the journey to Estradia reminding himself that some things were impossible.

Isla was behind him now, and he had to leave her there.

The shuttle slid into the belly of the flagship, and Elijah tore himself from his reverie.

Enough wallowing in thoughts, in fruitless desires, and a past he couldn't change. He had to focus on the present—on dealing with Lucas.

The rustle of releasing safety catches on harnesses filled the cabin, and Elijah unclipped his own belt before placing his helmet on. Rising to his feet, he put his hands before him, waiting passively while one of Grav's team fastened steel manacles around his wrists.

And as the restraints clicked into place, Isla's parting words whispered to him. *You instinctively understand what it takes to rule well. That's not weakness, that's what true strength is ... so embrace who you are.*

Warmth suffused his chest then. Isla would never know just how much she'd moved him. Her opinion mattered to Elijah, and he'd never forget the promise he'd made her.

Lucas's wrist-comm started to vibrate as he took the elevator down from the command deck. Glancing down at the screen, he frowned before opening the encrypted call. "Nix," he greeted the commander. "Do you have an update?"

Flanked by two battle-droids inside the elevator, Lucas had enough privacy to speak openly. He wouldn't have taken the call if *Dominion's* officers had been present—none of them were aware that he'd employed Nix and his special ops team to eliminate his brother.

And since some of them would have turned on him if they knew, they'd never find out.

Nix had required assistance on Estradia, after his assassination attempt went wrong, and Lucas had provided him with a squad of twenty battle-droids. That should have been sufficient to hunt down Elijah—but it hadn't been.

"Negative, Sir," Nix's voice, low and edged with fatigue, replied. "The chaos in Crelcaster has made a search difficult … and we've turned up nothing." The commander paused then. "I'd wager they *were* on that freighter that took off without clearance four days ago."

Lucas's jaw clenched.

He should have known Nix would bring that up—anything to take the focus off his own failure. At the time, the marine had suggested that Elijah had somehow found an ally at Crelcaster spaceport and managed to secure passage off-planet.

But Lucas had been sure his brother was hiding out somewhere in the capital.

He'd always known Elijah was resourceful, yet even he had his limits. He didn't have funds or any means of communication. However, he *was* desperate.

Swallowing down anger, Lucas sucked in a deep breath. Within moments, the elevator would slide to a stop and the doors would spring open. He couldn't linger over this conversation.

"What do we know about that cargo ship?" he asked.

"The *CS Intrepid* is a D-Class freighter … owned by a trader named Greta Mir-Hamil." Nix halted a moment. "She uses a few aliases as well, it seems … but there's a warrant out for her in two systems for smuggling."

Lucas's mouth pursed. He didn't see how the smuggler could be connected with his brother, yet it was the only lead they had. "All right then," he sighed. "Shift your focus to the *CS Intrepid*. I want that freighter found … and its pilot interrogated. If she helped Elijah get off Estradia, I need to know where she took him."

"Yes, Sir," Nix replied.

The elevator slid to a smooth halt then, the doors whispering open. Two security officers stood to rigid attention in the corridor beyond—awaiting their commander's arrival. Lucas tapped the screen of his wrist-comm, cutting the transmission.

"My Lord," one of the ensigns greeted him, slapping his clenched fist over his breast in the Mir-Ferrin salute. "Commander Grav and his team have arrived."

Lucas nodded. "Where is the prisoner?"

"In Cell-block 5E … Doctor Chisil is waiting for you before beginning the interrogation."

"Good to hear," Lucas grunted.

These religious extremists were a complication Lucas didn't need. He wanted to focus on finding Elijah and stirring up the Mir-Brennans. However, the *Creed of Truth* was fast developing from a nuisance to a threat to stability. Even though they'd arrested the leader of the Crelcaster attack, they still hadn't regained full control of Estradia's capital.

Striding past the officers, Lucas headed down the stark-white corridor toward *Dominion's* detention area.

After his call with Nix, and the frustration and worry of knowing Elijah was still out there, at large, Lucas needed something else to concentrate on.

His mouth thinned then. The rebel leader might have resisted Grav's methods of interrogation, but he wouldn't last long once Doctor Chisil started on him.

Cell-block 5E was a short walk away, over a series of catwalks that crisscrossed the detention area. A cool wind, laced with ozone, tugged at Lucas's clothing as he crossed the last of the slender bridges, the ensigns and his two battle-droids at his heels.

He found Doctor Chisil Mir-Ferrin waiting for him outside the largest of the interrogation chambers. The woman, small and elfin faced, was an unlikely-looking torturer. Yet appearances were deceiving. He'd met few people as 'methodical' as her.

Beyond a wall of one-way glass, he spied Grav and four members of his security team—two battle-droids and two cyborgs—flanking a figure dressed head-to-toe in black. A gleaming helmet covered the man's face. A large padded chair and a metal bench covered with an array of interrogation equipment sat behind the prisoner.

Lucas drew to a halt, frowning. "What's this?" he greeted the doctor. "Why aren't you in there ... and why isn't the prisoner strapped down and ready to go?"

The doctor pulled a face, her gaze flicking over the group assembled inside the interrogation chamber. "Commander Grav insisted on waiting until your arrival," she replied. "He refused to let me touch the prisoner ... or remove his helmet."

Lucas's frown deepened. Grav was a nuisance. Lucas had promised himself he'd get rid of him once he officially assumed his brother's seat, and he would.

"All right, Doctor, let's get on with it." He motioned to the chamber doors. "After you."

The woman tensed. "My Lord," she murmured. "There's something odd about all of this ... I suggest—"

"*After you*, Chisil," Lucas growled, cutting her off. He was rapidly losing patience with the doctor's dithering. "Let's see what our prisoner has to say."

Casting him a reproachful look, Chisil drew herself up, smoothed her palms on her white coat, and swept past him into the chamber.

Lucas cast a look at his battle-droids and ensigns that accompanied him into the block. It was already a bit crowded in the chamber. "Wait here," he barked before following at his interrogation specialist's heels.

But no sooner had the doors shut behind him when the manacles binding the prisoner's wrists fell away, clattering onto the floor.

Doctor Chisil gasped, halting abruptly.

Lucas reeled backward, his palm slamming onto the panel next to the door. On second thoughts, he *did* need his battle-droids with him in here.

However, the door remained sealed.

Lucas scowled, punching the panel once more, panic kicking him in the guts.

Meanwhile, the black-clad figure standing in the center of the interrogation chamber reached up and lifted the helmet from his head.

And when he saw the man's identity, Lucas's breathing caught.

His elder brother met his eye across the room. Elijah's face was impassive as he greeted him, "Hello, Lucas."

Lucas's heart lurched. His mind whirled, even as his gaze snapped to Commander Grav. *Bastard!*

Elijah took the laser-pistol the commander passed him and raised it, leveling the barrel at Lucas's chest. He then nodded to the members of Grav's security team standing nearest to his brother. "Arrest him."

His brother's words caused the shock that momentarily froze Lucas to the spot to shatter.

He wasn't going to let Elijah take him prisoner.

He shoved Doctor Chisil at the cyborg who moved his way, its blank gaze spearing him. The woman cried out, colliding with a wall of muscle and steel while Lucas dodged sideways.

He then drew the laser-blade he always carried at his hip, ignited it, and lunged for his brother.

But he never reached him.

A bolt of white laser exploded from Elijah's laser-pistol, striking Lucas in the chest.

29. TREADING WATER

"MY BROTHER IS dead."

The announcement echoed through the clan-lady's solar.

Standing near the windows that looked north across Briscay, Isla's gaze remained locked on the holo-image above Jenna's desk.

Eljiah Mir-Ferrin was focused on the clan-lady; he likely didn't even know anyone else was in the solar with her.

Nonetheless, Malik and Vic were also present. Like Isla, they stood back from Jenna, letting her conduct this meeting with the Mir-Ferrin clan-lord.

Isla drew in a shaky breath. Elijah was every inch the clan-lord this morning too. Clad in a tailored bronze tunic and black pants, a flowing bronze cloak hanging from his shoulders, his dark hair swept back from his face, he looked far removed from the man she'd said farewell to a week earlier.

And yet, the deep, smooth timbre of his voice was the same.

It still made her heart race and her belly flutter.

"I'm onboard *Dominion*," Elijah continued. "I tried to arrest him, but when Lucas went for me with a laser-blade, I killed him."

His voice was flat, yet Isla caught the way his gaze shadowed. Elijah had done what was necessary, but it had cost him.

"It's over then?" Jenna replied. Her tone was guarded. Despite that she'd spoken to Elijah at length during his time at Castle Valnor, despite that he'd signed a treaty between them, she still didn't trust the Mir-Ferrin clan-lord.

Isla didn't blame her.

Words were easy, as were agreements. It was actions that mattered.

This was the critical moment. Would Elijah prove that he was a man of his word, or would he drop the act and reveal his cooperation had merely been a ruse?

Isla's pulse accelerated, and she wiped damp palms on her leggings. Despite that she'd been sure of Elijah when he'd departed, had changed her mind entirely about him, doubt suddenly crept in.

What if he'd played them all?

"It is," he replied, his voice lowering. "But I've not forgotten what I agreed … as soon as I return to Platinum 5, I shall call a meeting with my commanders and governors. Changes will be made." He paused then before heaving a deep sigh. "However, I've got some damage to repair here in the Velix System. Lucas managed to upset quite a few people … I need to reassure the citizens of the buffer zone that they are no longer under any threat from my clan."

Isla exhaled sharply.

Likewise, Jenna's relief was palpable. The tension eased in her shoulders, and she nodded. "Thank you."

Their gazes held before Elijah's mouth quirked.

Isla's pulse quickened. Gods, how she'd missed that smile.

He'd only been away a week, yet seeing Elijah standing there—as real as if he were actually in the same room as her—made her long for him.

Curse it, why couldn't she let him go? She really had to. Elijah had returned to his old life, his old position.

He'll have forgotten me, already, she told herself. However, the ache under her breastbone increased at the lie. She knew he hadn't. He'd asked her to marry him, after all.

"Thank *you*, Lady Jenna," he replied. "Without your help, I'd have found it much harder to get to Commander Grav."

"He came through for you then?"

Elijah's smile widened, his dark eyes warming. "He did."

His gaze shifted slightly, as if he was trying to scan the space behind Jenna.

Isla's heart started to pound hard. *He's looking for me.*

However, the comm focused on Jenna alone, and it wasn't appropriate for Isla to step forward and interrupt them.

Elijah's attention snapped back to Jenna as he refocused once more. "You *all* did," he rumbled, "and I will never forget it."

Isla glanced up, her arm slung around Bea's shoulders, her gaze roaming over the rounded curves of the gleaming Lazda steel fuselage of the freighter parked before her.

"Very nice," she murmured, glancing over at where Aria and Vic stood a few feet away.

"It looks brand-new," Bea observed.

"It is," Vic replied, a glint in his eye. "Meet *The Wayfarer II*."

"Jenna contributed to the funds we'd saved," Aria added, grinning. "So, we decided we might as well buy ourselves something decent."

"Well, since Vic had to sell his last ship to get you both to safety … after I sent you into danger … it was the least I could do." Jenna's voice carried across the hangar. Isla turned to see the clan-lady approaching, Malik at her side.

Obsidian moved past Jenna and her husband, carrying a metal trunk up onto the landing pad toward the ship's open hatch. "That's the last of the supplies," the black battle-droid informed Vic.

"Thanks," Vic replied. "Go ahead and make the pre-flight checks."

Obsidian nodded. The droid's rubber-soled feet thumped up the ramp before it stooped to enter the freighter.

Isla smiled at Jenna. Of course, she and Malik would both be here to send Vic and Aria on their way.

Stopping next to Isla, Jenna's mouth lifted at the corners. However, her brown eyes were solemn. "I understand why you're doing this," she said, meeting Vic's gaze. "And I'm grateful for everything you've done for me over the past two years … but" —her gaze flicked to Aria— "don't be strangers. You'll always have a home here."

"Thank you, Jen," Aria murmured, her green eyes glistening with sudden emotion. "That means a lot."

"Can you take me with you?" Bea piped up then.

Isla snorted, giving her daughter's shoulders a gentle squeeze. Bea had Cathal's impatience. "I don't think so," she admonished her.

Aria drew close before reaching out and taking Bea's hands in hers. Seeing the affection on the woman's face, Isla's chest constricted. In the time since Aria had come to live at Castle Valnor, she'd become part of the family. She'd also spent much time with Bea, especially in the months during Isla's absence. "One day … when you're old enough … you're welcome to come on a trip with us." Aria's gaze flicked up to Isla's, as if checking it was all right to make such an offer.

Isla smiled. It was.

She'd always been a free spirit, and she certainly would never check her daughter. Once Bea was of age, she could go where she wished and be whomever she chose.

"Stay in touch," Isla replied, still smiling. Her attention flicked to Vic then, and she winked. "Like Bea, I wish I were going with you."

Vic huffed a laugh, even if his face remained expressionless. "Contrary to how it seems, we're not going on a jaunt. We're going to be *working*."

"Of course, you are," Malik quipped. "Just try to stay out of trouble, Mir-Riorde."

Isla smiled as Vic flipped Malik a vulgar gesture, while Malik just laughed.

Suddenly, she felt a pang of envy for Aria and Vic. They were taking action, moving their lives on. These days, she felt as if she were treading water. She felt as if she lacked purpose. Work on the new Mir-Brennan Tower on Idral was progressing well. Jenna and Malik would be moving there within the next month or two—and Isla and Bea were going with them.

But Isla couldn't get excited about the move.

She couldn't seem to dredge up enthusiasm for much these days. In the month since Elijah Mir-Ferrin had exited her life, she'd been restless, on edge.

Goodbyes were never easy, and neither was this one. It passed with the usual flurries of hugs, handshakes—and tears—before Vic and Aria followed Obsidian into *The Wayfarer II*.

The hatch sealed shut with a hiss, and the engines rumbled into life moments later.

"Listen to that," Malik murmured appreciatively, running his eye over the freighter as if he were gazing at a beautiful woman. "She purrs."

Jenna's mouth quirked. "You sound jealous … do you wish they were taking you with them too?"

Malik smiled down at his wife. "No … but there's something appealing about that sort of freedom. Don't you agree?"

Jenna sighed before nodding.

Meanwhile, the freighter lifted off its landing pad and rotated toward the open doors.

Watching it, Isla remembered the last time she'd stood here, almost exactly in the same spot, seeing Elijah off.

Her chest tightened at the memory. She wondered how he was—if he'd settled back into his old life, or if he felt as restless as she did.

The Wayfarer II accelerated out of the hangar, and shot up into the pale-blue sky, disappearing into a pinprick.

And just like that, Vic and Aria were gone.

The farewell party made their way out of the hangar, taking the long passageway that led into Castle Valnor's outer bailey.

Malik walked ahead with Bea as he told her, not for the first time, about how he and Vic had met, on the moon of Morith over three years earlier. He and Jenna had hired the cyborg to help them rescue Cathal, Isla, and Bea from Mir-Brennan Tower.

Meanwhile, Jenna and Isla trailed behind.

"I'm going to miss them both," Jenna admitted softly.

Isla glanced at her sister-in-law, noting her shadowed expression. "So will I," she replied. "Yet we both knew this day would come."

"We did."

"Have you found a replacement for Vic yet?"

"Not yet … I've got two candidates to interview tomorrow though."

The two women fell into companionable silence, following Malik and Bea into the outer bailey—a large courtyard that wrapped around the outer edge of the fortress. Potted trees and shrubs, and climbing vines, surrounded them, while the tinkle of fountains echoed against stone.

They'd almost reached the large sweeping granite staircase that led up to the main doors when Isla spoke up. "Have you heard from the Mir-Ferrin clan-lord of late?" The question was asked casually, even though her pulse quickened. Elijah had been on her mind a lot over the past days, and curiosity got the best of her.

Jenna cast her a sharp look. "Yes, as it happens. I had a call with him this morning. He's opened the shipping lanes again … for the first time in three years, we can now trade into Mir-Ferrin territory again."

Isla smiled. "He's still proving he can keep his word?"

"It seems so." Jenna's gaze fused with hers then. "Have *you* been in touch with him?"

Isla shook her head.

"Why not?"

"What would the point be?"

The clan-lady's mouth lifted at the corners. "You're clearly missing him." She paused then. "None of us can help whom we fall in love with, can we?"

Isla's breathing caught, and when she answered, her voice was strangled. "I'm not in love with him."

Jenna merely smiled, her gaze knowing. "Aren't you?" She exhaled sharply then. "You haven't been yourself ever since he left … you're distracted, and when you think no one's looking, it's as if you're far away." Jenna paused, her smile turning rueful. "I've reviewed my opinion about Elijah Mir-Ferrin. For what it's worth … there are far worse men to give your heart to."

Isla swallowed. "Okay, so maybe I do love him. It changes nothing though, does it?"

They lapsed into silence as they started to climb the steps.

"Elijah asked after you yesterday," Jenna admitted then.

Isla's pulse quickened. "What did you tell him?"

"That you were well."

Isla dragged a hand down her face before murmuring an oath. "He proposed to me, you know? When we said goodbye … told me there would always be a place for me and Bea at his side."

Jenna cast her a surprised look. "Did he?"

Isla nodded.

"And were you tempted?"

"I was."

"And now?"

"Gods damn the bastard … I can't let him go."

Jenna heaved a deep sigh before favoring her with a soft smile. "Well then, it sounds as if you have a decision to make."

30. FIERCE, WILD, AND BEAUTIFUL

THE HEAVY PADDED fist of the sparring-droid struck out, catching Elijah in the solar plexus.

Winded, he staggered back, side-stepping as the droid took a step forward and swung at him again. He blocked the next blow, yet his opponent was relentless this morning. The following punch caught him hard in the belly.

Elijah sprawled back, landing heavily on the padded mat.

Meanwhile, the sparring-droid loomed over him, its gaze pinning him to the spot. "Disabling blow delivered," it announced.

Grunting a curse, Elijah rubbed his throbbing mid-section. It had been a while since the sparring-droid had thrashed him like that. "Gods," he muttered. "I must be losing my edge."

"No, My Lord," the droid replied tonelessly. "However, you let your guard down at two critical moments. If you'd like, I can produce a detailed report on our fight and the errors made."

"Thanks," Elijah growled, rolling to his feet. "Send it through to my wrist-comm … you can return to your station now."

The sparring-droid bowed its head, turned, and strode back to its charging station, long arms swinging at its side.

Elijah watched it go, his mouth thinning.

Of course, he didn't need a report to tell him what he'd done wrong. It wouldn't tell him the reason—although he knew that too.

He was distracted.

He'd been back on Platinum 5 for over a month, had settled back into his old life, only to find that everything had changed.

For one thing, he was on his own now. His only remaining sibling was dead, by his hand. He had no other family left, save for a few distant cousins on his mother's side, who lived on a remote planet on the fringes of Mir-Ferrin territory. He hadn't seen any of them in years.

Elijah's days passed much as they had before that fateful day Lucas had sabotaged *Defiance*—he rose early and trained hard before spending his mornings in briefings with his commanders. He ate his lunch alone and then returned to work. There was much to be sorted out these days. They'd managed to restore peace to Estradia, yet those responsible for the uprising had disappeared.

There had been more problems in his territory with pirates too, and he'd had to deal with a handful of governors who'd reacted badly to the news they were now allies with the Mir-Brennans. The governors in question had been removed from position and replaced with those more open to peace.

Elijah had achieved much over the past weeks, but it had been exhausting.

And at the end of the day, he usually paid a visit to the rec-deck, where he took a run through one of the gardens before he returned home and ate dinner— alone.

Once, Elijah had enjoyed his routine, for he'd been focused on ruling well.

These days, he felt hollow at the end of the day.

The evenings were the worst, for they left him too much time to think—to torture himself with thoughts of Isla.

The other day, during one of his regular calls with Lady Jenna, he'd caved and asked after her.

The clan-lady had replied politely, telling him that Isla was well, and that she'd pass on his regards. However, he'd seen the glint in Jenna's eye. It was as if she'd seen straight into his head and knew just how desperate he was for Isla.

Heat had suffused his chest then, and he'd been grateful he wasn't one to blush.

Grimacing at the humiliating memory, Elijah moved off the mat, grabbed a towel, and wiped the sweat off his face, neck, and upper arms. He then grabbed a canister of electrolytes and took a swig.

Right now, he just wanted to stand under a hot shower.

He was heading toward the doors of his private rec-facility when his wrist-comm buzzed. The display let him know the call was coming from Platinum 5 spaceport.

"My Lord," a female voice greeted him. "Apologies for disturbing you so early ... but we have a woman here at Arrivals requesting an audience with you."

"Well, she can take a number," Elijah muttered under his breath, continuing his way to the bathroom. Everyone wanted a piece of him these days.

"The woman says it's urgent, My Lord," the comms-officer replied, her tone apologetic. "But I can tell her to go through the formal channels, if that's what you'd prefer?"

"What does she want?"

"She says you made her an offer, My Lord." The officer's voice was deeply apologetic now, "and she wishes to accept it."

Elijah skidded to a halt. "What?" he gasped, even as his pulse kicked into hyperdrive.

"I really am sorry about this," the comms-officer muttered. "You clearly know nothing about this. I shall—"

"What's her name?"

A pause followed. "Isla Mir-Brennan. She's traveling with her daughter."

A smile split Elijah's face. "And where's she now?"

"At the comms-desk here in the Arrivals terminal."

"Keep her there ... I'll be down immediately."

With that, Elijah cut the call and took off at a run toward the doors.

The woman took off her headset, her gaze settling on the woman and girl standing before her. "You're to wait here," she informed her. "It appears the clan-lord is coming down to fetch you, himself."

Isla nodded, keeping her expression sanguine, even if her pulse had just gone berserk at this news. "He is?"

"Apparently so."

The comms-officer ran her gaze over Isla, as if trying to fathom who she was, and why Elijah Mir-Ferrin would make a special trip down to the spaceport to see her, instead of sending aides or droids to do it.

Isla didn't enlighten her.

However, she was grateful for her assistance—even if the woman had taken some persuading.

"Thank you for contacting him direct," she said, smiling. "I appreciate it."

The comms-officer gave her a brisk nod before shifting her attention to the clearly impatient Gibbit waiting in the queue behind her. "Yes, how can I help?"

Realizing that she'd been dismissed, Isla took Bea by the hand and drew her away from the desk.

They didn't go far though, as they were towing large suitcases behind them, and Elijah had instructed them to stay put.

Bea flashed her a nervous, yet excited, smile. Finally, they'd gone on the adventure her daughter craved. A couple of days earlier, after her honest conversation with Jenna, Isla had sat her daughter down and explained her feelings for Elijah. She'd also asked Bea how she felt about moving to Platinum 5.

If Bea had been opposed to this move, she'd never have done it.

She needn't have worried though, for her daughter had surprised her. "Auntie Jen and Uncle Malik will be moving back to Idral soon," she'd replied, her blue eyes huge on her elfin face, "but I want us to make a new start." She'd paused then, her gaze never leaving her mother's. "And I want you to be happy."

Isla wanted to make a fresh start too. She no longer had a role amongst the Mir-Brennans. As Cathal's consort, she'd also been his advisor, as Malik was to Jenna. Initially, after her husband's death, she'd filled her days with rigorous training and plotting her revenge. However, ever since Isla's return to Staturine II, she was impatient to feel useful again.

"Are you scared, Ma?" Bea asked then.

Isla grimaced. "Terrified."

"Why?"

"I didn't tell him we were coming," she admitted with a sheepish smile. "What if he isn't pleased to see us?"

Bea rolled her eyes, as she was dealing with an idiot. "Of course, he will be."

Her daughter swiveled then, her gaze traveling across the gleaming bronze floor of the spaceport's Arrivals terminal. A huge transparent dome stretched overhead, giving them a clear view of the star-sprinkled void beyond. It wasn't overly busy this morning; they'd spot Elijah the moment he entered the terminal. "Where *is* he?"

"Alpha Deck is some distance," Isla replied. "It'll take him a while to get here."

Indeed, Platinum 5 was vast. The station was a stack of gleaming silver wheels mounted upon a central core. It orbited the unhabitable class H planet Formidian and consisted of five decks: Alpha, Beta, Gamma, Delta, and Omega.

Alpha, where the clan-lord resided, was the top wheel, while the spaceport was located on Omega Deck, at the base.

Isla knew he'd need time to reach them. But that didn't stop her, like Bea, from watching the doors.

And when a tall man with flowing dark hair, clad in black, strode into the terminal, Isla stopped breathing.

"There he is," Bea squeaked. She then started waving madly.

Spying mother and daughter, Elijah flashed them a broad smile and headed across the wide floor toward the comms-desk.

Isla stared at him. Her feet were cemented to the floor.

Jidea give her strength, he was dressed as he had been the first time she'd seen him—on the day she'd planned to end his life—in close-fitting black exercise pants and a sleeveless tank top.

He looked as if he'd come straight from a run or from the rec-facility.

Isla's heart started pounding in her ears.

Gods, she was suddenly transported back to that fateful day upon *Defiance*, when she'd raised that laser-pistol and prepared to end Elijah's life.

And now, here she was, prepared to marry him.

The enormity of everything they'd been through, and the fact they'd reached this point, cemented her feet to the floor.

"Go on, Ma … I'll look after our luggage." Bea tugged at her sleeve. "Don't just stand there!"

Shaking herself free of her reverie, Isla obeyed her daughter. Letting go of her suitcase's handle, she walked out across the floor toward Elijah.

They met in the center of the Arrivals terminal, drawing to a halt just three feet apart. Travelers swirled around them, yet neither Elijah nor Isla paid them any attention.

Elijah's gaze roamed over her face, his smile fading. An intense, searching expression replaced it. "Isla," he whispered. "You came."

Her mouth curved. "I did."

"Does this mean you accept my proposal?"

"If it still stands?"

"Of course, it does."

He closed the gap between them then, hauled her into his arms, and swung her around—and when his mouth slanted over hers, joy sang in Isla's heart.

Their surroundings faded. All she could focus on was the heat of his mouth, the taste of him, and the strength of his arms around her. Reaching up, Isla wrapped her own arms around his neck, melting into him. And when Elijah set her down, when he finally lifted his lips from hers, her vision had blurred.

He raised a hand and wiped away a tear that escaped with the pad of his thumb. His own gaze shone as he smiled down at her.

"I'd given up hope," he admitted softly. "I never thought this day would come."

"Neither did I," she replied huskily before flashing him a rueful smile. "Dammit, Mir-Ferrin, how did I go from wanting you dead, to falling in love with you?"

Emotion rippled across his face, and he swallowed hard. "I'm not sure … but I'm glad you did." He paused then, his mouth quirking. "So, you're in love with me?"

She reached up, her fingers entwining with his. "I have been for a while, I think. I was just afraid to admit it to myself."

He raised an eyebrow. "And you're not afraid anymore?"

"I just admitted to Bea that I'm terrified … but I wasn't going to let that stop me."

Isla glanced over her shoulder then, at where her daughter stood—dressed in her favorite purple cape, white jumpsuit, and high boots—watching their reunion. She wasn't sure how Bea would react to seeing her kiss another man that wasn't her father, yet Bea was smiling.

Catching her mother's eye, she waved.

"Beatrix looks happy to be here too," Elijah noted.

"Oh, she is … she insists we need a fresh start." Isla shook her head then. "I swear that girl has an old head on her shoulders."

"Just like her mother." The warmth in his voice, the affection, made Isla's belly flutter. She turned back to

Elijah to discover that he was gazing down at her, tenderness suffusing his face. "You are fierce, wild, and beautiful … a force of nature that no one should ever try to tame."

Isla smiled once more. She then reached up, her hand cupping his face. "And now, I'm *yours*," she whispered.

EPILOGUE. JUST THE BEGINNING

One month later …

ISLA HAD BEEN just twenty-three when she married Cathal Mir-Brennan. Ten years later, she took another husband and became a clan-lord's wife for the second time.

Both she and Elijah would have preferred a private wedding with limited numbers, but tradition dictated otherwise. As such, they were married on Platinum 5, in the Great Hall—a vast space at the heart of Alpha Deck. Lined with bronze columns, with a sweeping clear roof arching overhead, it was an impressive venue indeed. And it was just as well they'd chosen such a large space, for a huge wedding party filled the hall. A sea of brightly-colored robed figures covered the white marble floor.

Despite that she wanted to become Elijah's wife, Isla was nervous about her wedding day. It felt odd to make preparations again; it reminded her that she'd been a different woman a decade earlier.

She was also worried that her parents wouldn't attend, yet they did. They stood at the front of the crowd gathered before the raised dais, where a priestess to Miradia, the Goddess of Fertility and Marriage, performed the ceremony. As always, Isla's father wore a stern expression, while her mother stood regal and distant at his side.

It was hard to tell if they were happy for her or not. Nonetheless, her father was the Galbreth clan-lord, and such a union was advantageous to him. Isla hadn't told him the story of how she and Elijah had ended up together, or of the vendetta she'd sworn after Cathal's death.

Few people knew about that, and it was a tale best left behind them.

Standing opposite Elijah, she met his eye as the priestess's voice rang out through the hall. They were both clad in bronze, and Elijah wore a glittering badge with the Mir-Ferrin insignia—a crescent moon and twin crossed blades—on his breast. His dark hair was brushed out over his shoulders, and the cologne he wore was woodsy and fresh.

The scent settled her anxiety just a little, and Isla smiled up at him.

He winked back at her, his mouth lifting at the corners.

It was hard not to be on edge though, with so many eyes on them. Clan-lords and governors from all over the sector had made the trip to Platinum 5, for Isla and Elijah's marriage wasn't just a union between two people, but two clans. And unlike the last wedding between the Mir-Ferrins and the Mir-Brennans, which had ended in disaster, this wasn't an arranged marriage—but one of love.

Jenna and Malik attended too, as did Aria and Vic. The four of them stood in the front row, along from Isla's parents, with Bea.

The priestess was reciting the wedding blessing now as she unwrapped the bronze ribbon that joined their hands together. "May the best you have ever seen, be the worst you will ever see," she murmured. "May all evil sleep, and all good awake to pave your way through this life." The priestess stepped back then, allowing the clan-lord to speak his vows.

Elijah clasped Isla's hands in his and stepped close, his deep voice carrying high into the clear domed ceiling. "You are the star of every night. The face of my sun. And I promise to keep your heart safe till I draw my last breath."

Isla's skin prickled. She knew the words of the vows, had heard them and spoken them before. However, there was something about the way *Elijah* said them that made her breathing grow shallow.

Isla's own voice was hushed, husky, as she repeated the wedding oath.

Silence followed her words.

"Miradia be praised," the priestess said then, raising her arms, which glittered with bangles. "I declare you wed."

Elijah flashed Isla a grin, and her belly fluttered— even after a month of living with this man, he could still scatter her thoughts with just one look. He then bent his head, claiming her mouth in a lingering, tender kiss.

Cheering erupted within the Great Hall, thundering high into the dome, while the stars above twinkled down upon them.

Breathless, Isla and Elijah finally drew apart. Then, hand-in-hand, they turned to face the sea of guests.

Isla's parents looked as unmoved as earlier, yet Bea was crying. A frisson of alarm jolted through Isla at the sight, although when her daughter flashed her a wide smile, she realized Bea wasn't upset but overcome. Likewise, tears trickled down Aria's face, while Jenna brushed away her own. Malik was grinning, and even Vic appeared moved. His mouth twitched as he watched them.

Isla couldn't help it; she was suddenly grinning so widely that her face ached. Elijah's hand in hers felt right. *This* felt right. Over the past weeks, there had been moments when she'd worried that she'd taken a wrong turn. Old fears, old insecurities, had crept in. But now, as she stood at her husband's side, facing those who ruled the Rith Sector, she knew she hadn't made a mistake.

Loving Elijah had taken a lot of courage, yet she was glad she'd embraced what lay in her heart rather than running from it.

Tightening her grip on her husband's hand, she glanced across at him, meeting his eye. "This is it then, My Lord," she said as the cheering continued. "The old hates, the old feuds, are dead and buried."

His gaze, so dark it was almost black, glinted. "Yes … an era has ended," he murmured before a slow smile stretched his lips. "But for us, Isla, this is just the beginning."

The End

Here we are at the end of the epic GALACTIC CLAN WARS trilogy.

I loved writing these books, and hope you loved reading them too. Science Fiction Romance has always been a passion of mine, and I enjoyed bringing the Rith Sector and its warring clans to life in this series. There's nothing I like more than blending high-octane adventure, exciting new worlds, and steamy romance together—and I hope you agree!

If you can't get enough of this story world I've created, please drop me a line and let me know. I have many more exciting stories floating around in my head and would love to write them!

Samantha

Get in touch with me at: samanthajcharlton@gmail.com

GALACTIC CLAN WARS GLOSSARY

The three dominant clans of the Rith Sector

Mir-Brennan
Clan insignia: a shooting star above a clenched fist.
Clan motto: Glory is the reward of valor
Clan color: gold

Mir-Ferrin
Clan insignia: crescent moon and twin crossed blades
Clan motto: Righteous and devoted
Clan color: bronze

Mir-Lelith
Clan insignia: a silver full moon with a shooting star above it
Clan motto: We do not forget
Clan color: silver

Galactic gods

Jidea: Goddess of Fortune
Wis: the Seer of Truth
Aura: Goddess of Prosperity
Fara: Goddess of Light
Nain: Goddess of Darkness
Syr: God of Mercy
Raul the Destroyer: God of War
Miradia: Goddess of Fertility.
Examples of lesser deities: Bron the Worthy/Eldra the Wise

Technology and Weapons:
A pyro-grenade/pyro-torpedo: heat incendiary devices
Ardex: latex style material
cyan-shield: a glowing blue sphere that is triggered from a device strapped to the wrist
Klick: a term used to denote one kilometer or 1,000 meters

Laser-blade: a futuristic sword or dagger that consists of a grip with three settings. Blue is practice/spar, orange is stun, and white is kill

Laser-pistol or rifle: Energy output for practice is zero, fifty percent for stun and anything over eighty percent is lethal

Lazda Steel: highly durable metal

PCSD: a small Portable Currency Storage Device, which contains hard credits

Public Sectornet: a comms network publicly available throughout the sector

Shadownet: a comms network used by the criminal underworld

Wrist-comm: a small communication device worn on the wrist

Different classes of droids
Battle-droids
Utility-droids
Server-droids
Ticketing-droids

ABOUT THE AUTHOR

Samantha Charlton is a multi-award-winning author of Amazon best-selling Historical Romances, writing under a nom de plume. However, she doesn't just have a passion for the past, but also the future. She has had a lifelong love of Space Opera and Science Fiction. This led her to write stories—with high-adrenaline adventure, and emotional and steamy romance—of her own!

Connect with Sam online:
www.samanthacharltonauthor.com
www.facebook.com/samanthacharltonauthor
Email: samanthajcharlton@gmail.com